MELISSA COBB

MARRIED
TO THE WRONG
ONE

I0629732

Copyright © 2025 by Changing The Heart Publishing
All rights reserved.
No part of this book may be reproduced in any form without
permission from the author, except by reviewer who may quote
passages to be printed in a newspaper or magazine.

PUBLISHER'S NOTE

This book is a work of fiction. Names, characters, businesses,
Organization, places, events, and incidents are the product of the
Author's imagination or are used fictionally. Any resemblance of
Actual persons, living or dead, events, or locales are entirely
coincidental.

ISBN 13: 979-8-9931887-7-5

Printed in the United States of America

Married to the Wrong One

A Novel by:

MELISSA COBB

Thoughts of L. T.

"LIES ARE EASY FOR MEN TO TELL, JUST TO GET THEIR DICK WET."

There are many lonely women out there that will do just about anything for a man and his attention. They will dress tempting and provocative; slutty and if we address you as such; or fuck you as such we're the bad guy. It is true men of my nature do some hell of a shit just to get in your panties but that is a part of our dog ass nature. We see women and we talk shit. Point blank. Men will feed you bullshit all day long and tell you what you want to hear and not what you need to hear. In almost every case that shit we speak is good enough to get between your legs. If you really trying to prove a point, our dicks will get sucked in the process; stupid bitches when you ever going to learn?

As for my dogs, my home boys we chill other places. I don't bring them to my house because that is where I live. Women recognize that men are underhanded. I can be a damn dog ass Nigga and I do ensure dog ass shit. Men need to get it that no motherfucker needs to hang out at their house because real dog ass Niggas will come to your house, drink yo shit, eat yo food and fuck your woman. On top of that, if we want you, yeah we will keep at you until we succeed because if you want that bread; which, some have, we will exchange that bread in the form of paying your bills for that pussy. The bottom line is pussy can make yo ass or pussy can break yo ass.

As for you women, whenever you get it through your heads that we don't give two fucks, then our bullshit days are over but that does not seem to happening anytime soon. We will lie and even shed fake tears just to look believable, and the saddest part is we are laughing on the inside. On top of that, we will fuck you and all your friends, when ya let us. Then again all we have to do is pick out the one bitch that secretly hates on you and most of the time it's your entire click. When we discover this, we can fuck all y'all and won't shit be said because each bitch wants their turn to be dick down by another woman's man. Actually, it's the thrill of her not knowing that her man's fucking her girls too.

This works great until one of you becomes greedy and we all know that women really can't share dick like men can share pussy. You may think it is not cool for men to play games when it comes to emotions of a woman but shit the games y'all play are far worse. You say you don't fuck on the first night; get her ass drunk, you say don't suck dick; get your pussy lick and watch you return the favor and the best one of all is: you say you can fuck without feelings; bitch, fuck your ass good, hard and long enough; you fall in love.

Don't let you be the kind of woman that plays hard to get; if you are we take more pride in breaking your bitch ass down; just because we can. However, there are women out there that are gullible and they are what we call "All day suckers." By that they lap up everything they are told and will take care of us before they take care of their children; that's fucked up. Bitches, most men don't have their own damn money and those that do will fuck off yours just because you gave it to him. As for those that like to be hit, fuck you and many like you! Some men might but I don't have time to go to jail because of yo ass likes to be abused.

However, if you are the kind of woman that is needy or thirst for attention, men will fulfill your wish by being there every time you need to hear from them, take you out to eat and being your friend. The whole time we are acting like "that guy" we are wining and dining that ass. If you are the type of woman who craves attention, men will go far and beyond, to shower you with meaningless words and gifts. If by chance you have trust issues, we will demonstrate honesty and integrity just to win you over. Last of all if you desire a man to be a father figure to your children (meanwhile their own children go lacking), we will be that Nigga for you because all children like animals; I'm a dog, bow-wow motherfucker.

By that we will be thoughtful to the children and not you; just to deceive you into thinking we are not in it for the sex. Sadly, the misconception is it's always about the sex and how much of it we can get. We men think about sex as much as we breathe. It is when your ass is vulnerable or trying to be that bad bitch to take another woman's man is what makes the game worthwhile. Just to let you know, whorish men don't care too much if they have other women; it's only the wife they care for.

With regards we'll be the type of Nigga you looking for, by then you won't care either about that wife of the other women. The thing is you will think "It's good he has somebody that way he can't require a lot of your time." Wrong again, we just want that ass and however way we get it. We will sell you a dream; without the true cost of its worth. We don't care about you being hurt, what the fuck is that? We screw with our dicks not our heart or mind. We don't tell you to fall for us or the shit we tell you. It is your lonely looking for something, weak ass that does it. Women want a man to listen to them and we men will hear with our ears but our eyes are on your body; fuck that shit coming out your mouth.

3

Women want to be the center of our life we only want the center between their legs. Women desire to feel special, wanted, needed and all that other stuff in between. That is where dogs like me come in again, turn your world upside down and inside out by playing on your emotions and just like that; your ass is hooked thinking you have a good Nigga. For many women say they want a good man but fucking off with a married man or a taken man at that is not the way to think you possibly have a good man.

To me and millions like me, we have our own definitions of marriage and the way the words, I love you and just friends are taken. Various people do not think these words are real and in the generation of lack of tradition; they are absolutely right. Everybody is always looking for something, money, fortune and fame is the least; it's love, peace and somebody else's dick. Yeah, no one wants their own man, dick for that matter; they want what someone else has.

Nowadays money rules and all that mushy shit, comes last because if we lie to the other women, we will lie to you. What is a relationship anyway if the one you love is not faithful? What is faithful, if not too many people does it? What is communication if there is more fucking than talking? When does the "Just Friend's Theory" apply? It applies when the conversation goes no further than how you doing. People love according to the way they live. If they love at home, that is where their heart will be but if they love the streets; that too is where their heart will be.

I never thought I had to make a conscious decision about who I love or what I loved the most, but I did. It never occurred to me that what I love may never love me back. I only thought that if I hustled harder or got that money that I would be happy or we would be happier because we don't have to want. In regards, "Every one step forward, is two steps backwards" Now let me go back to where it all began.

CHAPTER 1

When it came to outsiders, The Times family doesn't care. If you owed them money and didn't pay; you paid in ass then you paid in cash. You can say the family I lived in was as hard core as they came. No one crossed any of The Times Family. If you messed with us, we put that Time on your ass; no questions asked.

My name is Lamar Times but everyone calls me L. T. and if they don't know me, they know about me and my family. You see we didn't just talk about it, we are about it. Growing up on the east side of town below the tracks; means you either be on your shit or get hit. From the time I was old enough to talk, all I ever knew were the streets. It is funny how other children were raised up saying their alphabets; I was raised up saying "Are you my hoe or my bitch?"

Starting out, I used to get arrested for petty stuff like; graffiti, fighting, sell charges and being a drop off Nigga; although, I got arrested one of the OG's would come for me. But when I got home, that would be my ass because I got trapped and the family look bad. It wasn't enough to get a beating because I got caught. With this fast life, also came fast women and I mean all types of women. No matter what kind of woman you wanted, she would not be hard to find because literally pussy would be at a Nigga. Every day of the week there was trim to get and it was not your average trim but "Grade A" pussy; we only mess with the best.

In this lifestyle, you fake it to make it because you were really making it. Whatever you wanted you could get it especially with the right connections and money. Once you tasted the life of doing what you want going back to lack is never an option. However, as I grew, so did my crimes. They became forgery, counterfeit money and my number one scheme: buy, sell and trade.

The leader of The Time family is my grandfather OG Pete. He was easy going but as mean as they come. When he and I would talk, he would never tell me what he was actually saying instead he would to tell me these old sayings which have stuck with me. On the other hand, if you came at him like somebody, he would address you as somebody. However, most of his business arrangements were friendly because he always tried to keep the peace. OG Pete used to always tell his followers that he can't make money if there was beefing going on; unless he ordered it.

Most of his posse consisted of about ten other OG's and when they would step on the scene, everything else subdued. Whatever OG Pete said, that is how it goes. His words were law of the land. Honestly, they weren't regular looking thugs. My grandfather and his crew looked like they worked in an office somewhere. They all wore suite, ties, brim hats and Stacey Adam shoes to match.

They all looked real respectable men, and I admired that look. OG Pete used to tell me that you must look descent no matter where you go; especially if you plan to conduct business. I never thought of selling Kilo's or running drugs as a legit business but that is the only business I ever known. He even spoke of my drawings as a business that could pay off if I let the right people get a hold to it.

There were a few people that crossed him. For the women, he didn't want money in return he wanted that pussy. For the men that reneged on their part, they paid dearly. With my own eyes, I have seen his men hang a man upside down and cut his dick off; then kick it around like the game hot potato while laughing.

OG Pete would have hits out on people that snitched on him or any of his members. In honesty, it was a blessing just to be a member of his gang. If you told people you ran with Pete's OG, they backed down and gave you whatever you asked. I loved that authority that he demanded on people. Somewhere along the way he got set up and was serving life for multiple hits and robberies. That is why my circle is limited, and I plan to keep it that way.

Before he left he said, "Boy get the hell out the game and away from Fat Girl. If you don't you will end up like me and you don't want that. These streets were here before you were born, and they will be here when you die. You can't beat the streets. Go to college and draw ya ass off. Get a legit business and rise above what we have taught you but always keep the hustler mentality Do you hear me?"

"Yes Sir." I replied.

He looked at me and spoke, "You don't hear shit because my daughter won't let you but mark my words, somewhere in your life you will change."

That was all he said and that was the last time I talked to him alive. The next thing I know he was out the game and dead as hell. When OG Pete, left the scene my Uncle Man-Man stepped up and became the boss. He also kept the crew together. In fact, he was the only one that Fat Girl didn't mess with. He had me picking up drops and even taught me how to use that baking soda for Caine. Easiest doe, I ever made. However, Man-Man was dirty. He would cheat anyone to get what he needed. I hand to learn the hard way. My own uncle set me up bait just so the main load could get by the FEDS. The shit was fucked up but he paid me well for that; even though, his ass got set up and died with a life sentence.

Now my mother, his daughter was known as Fat Girl and that was how I was to address her. If I called her momma, that meant my ass. She was a 5'6, dark skinned, stocky built and tatted from the tear drops by her eyes to the thorny rose on her ankle. She was the unshakable bitch nobody fucked with her. She would slap me around because she did not want me to be a weak mother fucker like my father. Speaking of my father, I don't miss his weak ass. He had a chance to rescue me from the life Fat Girl had for me but he chose to save his damn self. I could barely remember him.

"That bastard" *I said out loud.*

Getting back to my thoughts, Fat Girl would make me hit her. I don't mean tap. I accurately hand to hit her like she was a Nigga in the streets. Mind you that I never wanted to do that but she is mom and if she told me to swing, my ass better fucking swing. On a few occasions, I decided to take a stand. When she came at me to hit her, I didn't. It was the worst mistake I ever did. She would hit me until I hit back. It wasn't just that, she would make me angry, for her to get angrier. She provoked me sore until I angered.

9

Fat Girl did all that just so she could beat the hell out of me. There were days, that I didn't go to school because she kicked my ass over in the night; mainly because she was bored. Quite a few days she needed to feel that adrenaline rush and my ass was the only way for her to get that when no one else was around. My mother was the type of woman that I swore I would never marry. I never thought I would get away but when she died from multiple gunshot wounds, I saw that as my way out.

I thought about reality and how my I did get that Art Degree and how my wife Solo took me away from the life of making that behind the scene's paper. Before I decided to do my own thing, I wanted to see how an average Joe makes his bread. Therefore, I tried working for seven dollars and something an hour, but that shit was not doing it for me.

I did what I know and that was to get back in the money pool by changing my game. Now my wife didn't like women calling me or always in my face and I respected her for that. Therefore, my Body Shop mechanic business was in the front but in the back it is a chop shop, buy, sell and trade operation. What can I say, everybody needs a car fixed and or painted.

Breaking my chain of thoughts was the sight of my best associate in the world, Mudcat. I met him when he first got in the game a little over ten years ago. He needed to make some quick cash and he paid off to be the best investment that I ever made. He is my right hand nigga and the one that doesn't mind getting his hands dirty every once in a while.

Mudcat is the type of nigga that could fix anything with wheels, go in your house fuck your girl, steal your shit and help you look for your shit; all at the same damn time. Fuckers like that you would want to keep on your team and keep his ass close by. I know he knows just as much as I do, the only difference is I have the women, money and the connections.

Giving him the "What's up?" head nod I spoke, "Nigga let me show you something about two of my women."

"What's that?" He asked.

"One is a bitch, the other is a hoe: What's the difference if they both fucking?"

"Man, there is no difference if they both fucking" Mudcat replied.

"Wrong."

Opening up my cell, I text Lizzie.

"Where my pussy at?"

Seconds later she replied, "For snack, I am having a dick-nana split with extra Cool Whip topping and you will be served bagels (this ass), cream cheese (that cum) and my pussy on the platter, bon appetite!"

I showed him the response to the first one. I then spoke, "Watch this text."

I sent the next text to Dandy.

"Where my pussy at?"

She then responded, "Motherfucker, I got your pussy, pussy! If you don't think I won't make you nut think again, now come get it! "

Smiling, I showed him the text, and he laughed as I asked, "Now; which is which?"

"The last one, that's the bitch right there, ain't it?"

"Hell yeah, she likes to fight and get all ghetto, but she knows not to fuck with my wife. If any of them cause her grief they will answer to me and as for niggas like me hollering at her, they better bark and don't bite."

"Shit if they do, I'm helping you fuck them off. Nigga if any outside friendship bitch contacts yo main woman in any way, that bitch ain't good for nothing but to be pissed on" Mudcat spoke with much tone.

"All these women I chill with, I don't make love to any but Solo. These bitches, I hit them from the back because I don't need to look in their faces to fuck but if I have to I will."

"That's some true shit right there. If I'm on top of they asses they don't need to look all in my face and shit. I might spit on that bitch while she looking. Hell I'm not trying to plant a seed in those bitches, they just a nut. When they ever going to learn that taken men don't want they cheating asses?" Mudcat spoke with humor.

"They don't have to learn on my watch. I'm not trying to teach them shit."

At that moment, a youngster spoke from the window of a moving car saying, "You the man L. T. you the fucking man!"

Giving him a fake nod and a smile, I yelled back for no reason, "It is what it is, lil homie! It is what it is!"

"Man let me get back to putting this transmission in. I have a shorty I have to see and some nut to put down her deep as throat" Mudcat laughed as he walked off.

Soon as Mudcat walked off, I saw my wife staring out the window. A few seconds later she came out the door. Solo was wearing her strapless sun dress that stopped at her knees as her hair swung loosely about her neck. I could see the locket I gave her still intact, as she walked towards me, in her expensive sandals. The way her honey skin glowed, it made her penetrating brown eyes shine but the closer she got I saw something different. Solo's smile that usually lifts her eye brows now hung low. Her cell phone was in her left hand and when she got closer to me, she slapped me with her right hand.

Grabbing her up by the neck, I saw Mudcat run out the shop with a crow bar. I spoke in haste, "What you do that for! Huh, what the hell wrong with you!"

She only stared at me with many tears upon her beautiful face. I looked down at her hand and opened it. She revealed her cell phone and on it was a multimedia message. Pushing play, it was Lizzie, her twin sister Eliza's voice and when the guy started moaning, I knew it was me but had to play the shit cool.

"Get your lie together so you can tell me, it's not you I hear on this phone. When I know how you are. I know how you sound when the sex is good. Now look me in my eyes and tell me the truth!"

"Do you see my face on this bootlegged ass recording? Huh? Hell no you hear a voice. You come out her slapping me and over some bullshit that I don't even know about" I spoke sounding real as ever.

"Stop it! Stop trying to play me stupid. It's one thing to fuck off with Lizzie but her fucking twin too? Those low down bitches can't stand me and here is my husband banging the shit out of them. You a damn dog and I love the shit out of you but I am fed up with your whorish ass ways. Ever since day one when we met, I tolerated all kind of shit but to actually hear it with my own ears" Solo spoke as she cried harder.

"Baby you don't see anything but hear a voice, you think is mine. Could be one of those love sick bastards you work with at the office, disguising their voice to break us up. How do I know? They may play with the computer long enough and do all kinds of shit to make it sound like me because they want yo ass!"

She stopped crying. Solo began shaking her head to say, "You trying to flip this on me, but you can't because I have been faithful to you since the day we got together. No man has come at me and especially not on my damn job. It's beneath you anyway to try to turn the shit around on me. L. T. the fucking mind games you trying to play on me, doesn't work."

Damn she is getting good at this mind shit. I must have taught her well. I wanted to sit beside her but knew all too well. Solo got up and cried when she looked in my face. It tore at my soul to see her hurt. I do my shit, I can't lie but I always kept it from her. She has only ideas but no actual fact. This media message isn't really factual but it's too damn close.

"I'm just saying. You don't think pussy and dick want what we have? You don't think that men out there want to be with you just as much as women out here want to be with me? They can do all kinds of shit. Just like this untraceable and altered message."

"If it is altered, how does anyone know how you sound when you fucking but me, if I am the only one you have been with since we been together?"

"Men we play around by how we sound when we getting the goods. We say all kinds of shit because we men and yet we horse around like boys and any of them could have taped me or the next man. It is a cold cruel world out here and people don't like to see others happy. Misery loves company and we can't let this happen to us. But I will find out whoever is sending you shit about me, believe that."

She didn't act like she believed me, so I began to sound like I was crying. I needed to amp up my lie by saying, "I love the shit out of you and it pains me to know that you may not believe me, all because someone sounds like me on a damn tape. I thought we had a marriage built on trust and all that good shit but now you making me rethink that our vows meant shit."

"You know I believe you but something tells me that I shouldn't. Something tells me that you are lying and I should run."

"Look at me" and she did.

"Do you honestly think I would be out front and crying for anyone to see as they drive by, huh? Do you honestly think that I would be recorded making out with other women when I have all I need at home?"

"Babe no, I don't think you are that stupid?"

Deciding to up my performance to an all-time high, I began to let tears fall as I spoke, "Why would I lie to you? Our marriage is built on trust and we have no secrets. If I did something like that I would be the first to tell you that I fail and I am so sorry but I didn't do that. I love you So-nya Lo-wanda Times. I don't love those whores. I love you babe, I love you. I talk big boy shit to them, I do but that is far as it goes. You my world and to have my world upset pisses me the fuck off!"

"Calm down L. T. It's ok? I need to go away to my sister's anyway to clear my thinking and to sort out everything" Solo said as she stood up and gently took her phone.

"Everything like what?"

"I've been thinking about your way of living to begin with. I think you need to prioritize the things in your life."

"You are my number one" I stated in truthful as I pretended to dry the tears up.

"What about the streets, the women, the stolen goods, the fast money, the only way you know how to live?"

"It's all you first and all I do in these streets is for you. I do this shit so you won't ever have to want for anything."

"No, L. T. it's for you. I can love you and be just as happy in a small house and an ordinary ride. I don't need the expensive clothes, extravagant vacations, shopping sprees, the rich lifestyle you like. It's true, it has its advantages but when the sun comes up, it's all the same. I just need you and you don't understand that. You say you do but you don't. This way of living is all you have ever done and if I don't take a stand, it is all you will ever do."

"You just saying that because you have it. What if you didn't have it?"

"No I'm not. I don't ask for much."

"No you don't and that is why you should have everything you desire but would you still want little old me, if I didn't have anything?" I asked already knowing the answer.

"Yeah, I would still love little old you even if you can't afford to buy me the finer things."

We both paused for the ball was in my court. I knew that I could persuade her to stay but she is right. Solo does not deserve the way police could bust in at any time on us; even though, she deserved this way of living. She really desires to go away to think and I will not take that from her but I will try. Clearing up my tone more, I verbally I asked, "How long you think I would be without seeing you? You know I can't go too long without you."

"Maybe a month, maybe less, maybe more, who knows? When the time is right for me to come back home, it will really be a home and not a trap house."

I placed my arms around her and pulled her close. I know her. She is serious when she has that look in her eyes. Now I am about to go through a few months without having her in my bed and in my life. We won't be fucking, touching and none of that good shit. Fuck, who the hell has done this shit, I love this woman and to have her having doubts about me is something I won't have. There have been many instances, I talked my way out of some stupid ass shit and this is something small and she is leaving. It's something in the water.

"If you want to go to your sister's fine, get the fuck on" I lashed out at her.

"Why are you angry again?"

"I just get pissed because someone is accusing me of shit and I am not doing shit. Where I am when I am not out scouting for goods? At this damn shop painting my ass off or doing some type of work. These hating fuckers I wish they all die!"

"I only stated that I needed to get away to think. I have always thought of you as faithful and here I am listening to a voice that sounds identical to yours and you mad at me? How the hell you expect me to react?"

"I expected you to ask questions first. You can think right here at the house. You don't need to go to your nosey ass sister. You know she doesn't give a fuck about me and I her. She hates the fact that we got married."

"This isn't about what my sister likes and doesn't like. It's about us doing all we can to keep this marriage drama free and happy" Solo stated as he walked off from me and back towards the house.

CHAPTER 2

Mudcat rushed over as he wiped his greasy hands on his jumper to say, "What the hell just happened?"

"Man somebody trying to break up my home and I be damn that is going to happen."

"What happened?" He asked as moments later we both saw Solo pack her Tahoe.

"Check this out. Somebody used an untraceable app to send her a voice video of me fucking Lizzie and her twin Eliza."

"Wait, I know you tearing Lizzie ass up, left and right but her twin too? You lucky mother fucker. I have been after that ass for a minute."

"It was just a one night with her sister. The thing is you can't see me you can hear me moaning."

"Yo ass got convicted over a voice?" Mudcat asked as Solo drove out the driveway.

"Yeah. She believes that it may not be me and the tape could be altered but she still needs to think."

"Where she going?"

"She is going to her sister's house."

Mudcat lit his cigar because the mention of Solo's sister leaves a sour taste in his mouth.

"Before you say anything, I am on break but back to what you just said."

I glanced up at him and fanned the smoke; for he knows that I don't smoke and can't stand the smell. Coughing, I then stated, "Damn you choking me out."

He saw me fanning and stepped backwards, while placing the tobacco stick in the other hand he said, "Sorry about that. Go on."

"You and I both know since you broke her sister's heart, her ass don't like me because she thinks I had you to fuck ole girl."

"You did set the pussy up, remember?"

We both laughed as I replied, "I didn't tell you to sleep with her. Shit, I fuck her from time to time and I wanted you to chill while I fuck. You my right hand man and I needed you to keep her friend company."

"The way she was working that pole and rolling that ass, shit you try not to stay there and not want to tap that fine ass bitch."

"Well you do have a point because she works the man pole better; especially the way she makes each cheek bounce.

Now that's some freaky bitch shit!" I yelled out in remembrance of how many times she has ridden my dick before.

"Is there any woman this side of the state you haven't fucked off with? I mean seriously? You've got more pussy than I can count and that does not include before I got with you. "Mudcat asked.

"There are a lot of them I hadn't fucked off with. I love women period, short, fat, tall, skinny and any color. Pussy doesn't have a face just a set of lips" I spoke with laughter.

It's something about ghetto bitches or bitches that want to fuck other women's men. Those types of women will let you fuck them any kind of way because they trying to make sure theirs is the best. Little do they know, we just want a nut, fuck them at their best because they can't take the main woman's place?

By snapping his fingers, Mudcat said, "Come out of pussy land and tell me what you going to do about your wife?"

Smiling I spoke, "I'm going to do nothing. I'm going to let her have her time and when I get tired I'll bring her ass home. Until then I can have fun and keep on doing what the hell I want to do."

"Break time over, let me get back to work" Mudcat stated as he walked back to the shop.

I sat on top of the picnic bench and turned to my contacts. I came to Lizzie's number first. Dialing it, I await for her to pick up.

"Hello" was her sexy ass voice.

"What you got going?"

"What you want going?" Lizzie asked seductively.

"I need to know something."

"What you need to know?"

"Do you remember the night I fucked off with you and your sister?"

"I can't forget that night because she was taking more turns than I was on your dick. Why?"

"Well somebody sent a clip to my wife and she was pissed."

"What?" Lizzie said with surprise.

"Yes, I don't believe you or your sister did it but I need to know if you know?"

"Think about this. You always get the hotel room and when we come in we don't ever leave your sight. So how do we bug the room or set you up?"

She was right. I always get the room so shit like this won't happen, even if I use their money. There is no way for them to bug a random room and not to go as far as not to get my face on camera.

"You there?" Lizzie asked.

"Yeah. I need to see you tonight, can you make that happen? If you can't tell me, I will make other arrangements" I asked her.

"Shit yeah. Do I have to bring Eliza?"

I thought about that for a minute. Her sister is a damn freak and she will make the average Nigga fall her ass. After thinking about it I spoke, "Fuck it. You can bring her."

"Why the hell I have to bring her greedy dick ass? She wouldn't let me hardly get any of that nut out you the last time. I don't want to share that nut with her."

"You asked me about her. I didn't ask you about her. Your ass is the one I wanted to put time on not hers. If you think you gonna need help bring her because I have a lot of pressure built up and it just might take the both of you."

"Fuck her. I'm greedy too. I want that dick all to myself." "This time I am coming to your house and I'm fucking in your bed. No damn room."

"Tonight, I hope your ass fucks the way you demand" Lizzie said.

"Have I ever disappointed you?"

"If you did, you wouldn't be getting this ass as much as you do."

"Let me get off this phone and I'll see you later on tonight."

I hung up with her and went to the shop to do more invoices and filing. Mudcat was working hard on that transmission because he knows that payday is tomorrow, and he doesn't want to be doing much of anything on tomorrow. I couldn't blame him. He has a main woman that he gives almost all his doe to. He won't wife her because he said she was a trick we all used to fuck her. To a degree, he is right you can't wife a hoe and you can't love a bitch.

A few hours past and I finished with this week's paper work. All I do now is set back and write checks and pay bills. I laughed at Solo as she crossed my mind. She wants me to give up making money for us to live as comfortable as we do. Other than McDonald's her ass has never had a job until now and it's not because I wanted her too, she wanted to try it. I was cool with that because there was no reason to pay for an education that she wasn't going to use. Now she makes a little money and when I say little I mean six hundred a week, shit I make that in half an hour.

I love her and I stand by her like she does me. Smiling I decided to call her.

"Hey babe, I miss you even now."

"I miss you too."

Then the phone was silent. Breaking that silence she asked, "Do you really miss me and are you going to use this time to figure out what is important to you?"

"Hell yeah I miss my damn wife. I can't imagine sleeping without you, let alone knowing you are going to be gone from me for a short while."

The phone was silent again. She said, "L. T. I am serious. You need to take this time to discover what is important to you and I need to know that I am that important person to you."

"You don't think you are important to me?" I asked her seriously.

"I know I am important to you, but I don't compare to the money you make."

"It is you and not the money" I replied back to her.

"Is it? Then quit your behind the scene job, right now" Solo demanded.

The phone was silent, and I did not want to lie to her and from what she knows I seldom lie to her. My wife then spoke, "I know you are thinking when you are quiet."

I still did not respond because I was in no way going to give up this way of living because she wants me too. The money is too damn good and if I keep this up, I will be able to quit but not now, I want to stash out another half a million before I call it quits.

"That is what I am talking about. The life you live is more than I am to you."

"That is not true."

"Then tell me right now that you quit and I will come back home to you and we can start over."

"Solo I love you and being able to take care of you for life means more to me than you know. I promised you when I married you that I will take care of you. Let me do that. Let me get the weight I want and I will quit."

"What more is there? The house and all our vehicles are paid for. You have seven rental properties with brick houses on them which bring in about seven thousand dollars a month. The shop alone does well up to ninety-seven hundred a week if not more. God knows how much you have stashed back. If I know you like I believe I do, it's well over five million. So what is your excuse again?"

I was still quiet. She was right because she was my secretary until she decided to go to school and not be tied to anything that involved my behind the door operations.

"I'm quiet because I am going to miss you while you are away. I can't stop, not right now. I want us to continue to have what we need."

"You are all I need, L.T." She broke in to say.

"I know but if I can't make the money I need for you I will be almost angry with myself because no wife of mine will ever want or ask another mother fucker for shit."

"L.T., I know it's the way you were brought up. You know, I know because I have been with you since elementary school and I know it all was for you. Believe me, I love you and I don't need the fast life. You are addicted to it because it is all you ever done."

"I can't promise you overnight success, but do you remember the last time I decided to live honest?"

"Yeah, when we first got married and we didn't want to touch the savings so you got a job."

"Go on," I encouraged her.

She began to laugh because she remembered that we almost starved trying to live honest; even though, we had money saved we were trying to live like the average Joe.

"Why you laughing so hard?" I asked her.

"We almost starved depending on you to work."

"But look, we have our own body shop and we can eat steak every damn hour if you want to."

"I know."

"I will try to slow down while you are gone. Shit I don't think I can function with you not being here."

"I am sure Mudcat will make up for any loneliness you may feel."
"Mudcat doesn't have your wet, wet so he can't do a thang for me but shut the fuck up."

Solo laughed and it sounded so good to hear her laugh again like that. She hadn't been gone but a few hours and I miss the fuck out of her. I always go in the streets and do what I do but it's nothing like coming home to a woman that loves you for you. Without the money, these whores would pass me on to the next mother fucker. In hoping she would say yes, I asked anyway, "I can't come see you can I?"

"You know that will not be a good idea. How are you going to realize what you need, if you are always calling me or coming by to see me?"

"I knew you were going to say that, but I had to ask anyway."
"I know you know but you taught me remember."
We laughed and it seemed like we were not a part, but she was gone to visit her sister. She is laughing and talking to me. I got her now.

"Babe, your laughter is music to my ears."
"Stop feeding me some line."
We laughed again and I said, "For real, I miss your laughter, and I want you to know that I will be home until you

return and not just that but I might go to church with you."
"You have been thinking for you to want to go to church."

"Well, got to take it slow. Like you said but remember, I will fuck somebody up if they try to get my pussy."

"Could you stop? We are married and I don't chill like that and you know I don't."
"Got to remind you because you know, like you say the devil will tempt us when we are not with our spouse."

"Babe you do listen to me."
"I do and I know that women come to my shop all the time and it means so much that you trust me."

"I do but I just need you to get yourself together; while, I am away."
"I will. I am about to go get something to eat, then I will return to the crib to crash for the night. I'm going to hold your pillow tight and every night."

"Babe you get your priorities right and I will be there in person."
"Can I buy you gifts or send Mudcat by to check on you?"
Using humor, my wife said "No gifts before I ask for the moon."
"If I could buy that bitch, it's yours."
"That is what I love about you. You do all you can for me. You are such a great man and I don't want to lose you."

"How can you lose someone that won't get lost?"

"Good night babe. I need to go rest. I love you."

"Solo my love, I love you more."

We hung up. I locked up the shop and took a shower. Once that was done, I went to get something to eat before I visit Lizzie. Just that thought of that pussy got my dick hard. Thinking about skipping supper and go straight for desert, I texted her quickly,

"I'm on my way, have that pussy clean."

She replied, "K."

Bypassing Applebee's, I went uptown to Lizzie's rental brick house; which, she rents from me. Checking the time, I got out and knocked on the door. She opened it up wearing a black see through top, no panties and the smell of sex was all over her. I'm already, ready to dive in her body and I'm horny as hell. This bitch knows she looks damn good in black, too mother fucking good to be honest. If I wasn't married, I might have given this bitch a try because I'm the main one she fucking and her sex is almost top notch.

"You like" She spoke as she lightly kissed me on the lips.

"Girl do I like, shit I love it."

"Come on and let me take your mind off your troubles."

I needed to hear that shit because I have a lot going on with my wife leaving and shit. I needed a good fucking and a good night's sleep. She broke the embrace and led me into the bedroom. This scene is all too familiar to me. I've fucked in here many a days in this very same room, this very same house. She is the only bitch I will fuck bare and the only other pussy I will eat.

Sounds silly to fuck bare and eat out but I been fucking with her for a few years and I know she clean.

I give her everything she needs. She doesn't pay rent, light bills or anything like that. However, she pays her own cell phone bill and anytime I need her I get her, no questions asked. Lizzie knows if I catch her fucking up on me, I will break my foot off in her ass. Why would she have to cheat? She everything but my heart and that is something she can try to get but won't accomplish.

"L. T. relax and let me take care of you."

I smiled because she knows the kind of pampering I need after a hard day like today. I took off my shoes and placed them side by side. I stood up and she took off my tee shirt and slowly began to unzip my pants. I got undressed as she took my dick in her hands and slowly massaged him. She stepped back and turned around and from under the lacey shirt her perfect round ass was peeping at me. I loved the way they looked as she asked, "You sure you want this pussy tonight, I mean she is extra wet for you and if you can't handle it say you can't."

"Bring your ass to me."

She came over to me, naked and jumped up. I caught her light ass and we began kissing. I thought tonight why not give her what she been wanting from me. I'm in need and she stay in need, why the fuck not. Holding her ass in midair, I began to kiss her strawberry smelling body from her neck to her cleavage. Her breast is always my favorite as I allowed them to swallow my face with their aroma.

Lizzie began moaning as I laid her on the bed. The mood feels right as I began to skim my tongue over her nipples. I am not thinking about getting my dick sucked by her tonight. Oddly enough, I feel like taking her over and over and staying the night. I pulled away from her, stared into her eyes and said, "I've been fucking you for a few years and I care about you deeply. Tonight, I'm going to lay you on your back and fuck you like you should be fucked. No doggie style or you going for a ride. I need to stick some dick in your pussy, the way a man fucks the woman he cares for."

I hand never seen her smile so bright and to top it off, I did the new me. I went between her legs and tasted her. She was moist and sweet. I was getting out of control as I tasted her over and over. I never knew that another woman would make me feel like this and here I am finding out. The way she pushed on my head and the way she would squeeze told me she was in need of what I was giving her. I quickly got up, because I am now excited and in need to make love to her. It may be the worst mistake but I'm not thinking with my top head, my bottom head is in control and right now he wants Lizzie.

Positioning myself on top her, I glared into her eyes and she was about to close them. Quickly I said, "No, don't close your eyes. Stare into mine as I make passionate love to you."

She could not speak. She only nodded yes and wrapped her legs around my waist. Reaching down, I kissed her lips to sanction this love making act, I am about to perform to her. The very piece to and to it was her tasting herself upon my lips. Arching my back, I entered her slowly. Lizzie gasped like never before. I knew then that she was blown away by that very act alone and for me to make her stare into my eyes would be phenomenal.

Each time I took Lizzie she would gasp with pleasure and would not take her eyes off me. I kept telling her with each plunge of my dick into her, "This yo dick. Feel yo dick taking you.
This is some good as pussy. Girl you giving it to me, shit. I can't take this pussy. You are whipping the fuck out of me."

The psychological thing about that is, for her to see and hear who makes her feel the way she was feeling. I needed her to see that I am the man for her and the one in control of the way her body was reacting to mine. I had to say shit I would say to my wife and pretend to mean it, even if those words were lies. Yeah lies, I at some point pretended she was my wife and the pussy became awesome because no one fucks me like my wife and the bottom line is; I just needed a good ass nut.

It was working. The way she was meeting my every thrust, was beautiful. I had no idea that pretending to fuck Lizzie as Solo would make me feel this damn good. The more I pushed inside her, the deeper she pulled me. Lizzie's pussy tonight was awesome and the way she was throwing it back caused my rhythm to incline. She was staring at me; while, I stared over her. I only look at my wife in the face like that but tonight our bodies knew what the other one needed. No way was I pulling out the pussy and from the lock of her legs she wasn't letting me out anytime soon.

This fucking was intense as I ever and believes me; I've had pussy on top of pussy. I continued to stare pass her face because I knew her eyes were begging me to bury myself and they didn't have to ask anymore. I became glued as my dick became hung inside of Lizzie's body as she hollered out from her own orgasm. I finally looked into her face as the thumping of my dick stopped and her legs began to drop from my side. Words could not express the way the pussy got me tonight. Our breaths began to become normal. I pulled out of her and I rolled off onto my side of the bed.

We still did not speak. She laid in my arms and cuddle closer to me. We fell asleep and when I awoke the next morning, we were still in that position. I looked down at her as she slept and thought, *"Lizzie is beautiful but I have a wife and another woman on the side. I might have messed up by not pulling out and fucking her almost the way I fuck my wife. Damn! Fuck! I got fucking carried away and now my side chick is going to act like my main chick. I'll just be damned."*

Without looking at me Lizzie spoke, "I feel you tensing up. You don't have to worry about me wanting to take that wife of yours place. I know what we have and last night you made love to me the way you do her. I loved it. You have me wanting more of that loving."

"I am pleased you feel that way. Let us not talk about the life I have outside of you." I asked.

"You right but I do desire you to take me again like you did."
"I can't. I have to get to the shop and get things prepared for today."
"When you coming back?"

I stared at her. She has never asked that. She knows I come and go as I please and all of a sudden I make love to her once and now she has questions. Politely I reminded her, "You know I come and go as I please with you and I only answer to Solo."

Realizing that I better go shower Lizzie spoke before I could get all the way up, "But you didn't fuck her like that, you fucked me like that and that bitch can never have pussy like mine."

I yanked Lizzie so close to me that she could still smell her own pussy from my breath. I said, "Bitch! Don't you ever call my wife a bitch again, is that fucking clear bitch!"

Seeing the fear in her face and the tremble in her voice, Lizzie said, "I didn't mean it, L. T. You know that is just how I talk when I get upset."

"I don't give a damn how you talk when you are upset. You better curve that tongue when you mention her name and yo ass better not call her or do any damn thing out of the ordinary to her. Do you fucking understand me bitch!"

"Yes, I understand. I get it alright!" Lizzie spoke as I let her go.

Getting on up, I went to shower. She came in the shower and put her arms around me. She then spoke, "I'm sorry for that. I didn't mean to call her that."

I turned around and looked into her face for sincerity and it was there. Taking a sigh I replied, "Its ok, I just snapped when you call her that because if anyone is the bitch it's you because you fucking another woman's husband and can't get your own."

"If you stop cock blocking, I could find someone to have me but you always want my pussy to yourself. What if I get to sharing?"

"The day you share, is the day you start paying for all this shit you receive and want."
"What if I got pregnant? You don't think I am good enough to mother your children?"

"I wish the fuck you would. Yo ass better abort the motherfucker. Solo is the only woman I desire to carry my children."

"News flash, she can have all the children she wants but I give you what she can't."

"What's that?"
"Freedom to be you."
Lizzie was right as she got out the shower. My wife would never approve of me fucking other women and she would not have me out doing the things I do. On the other hand, Lizzie would. She knows this dick is too damn good to keep to myself and she knows I like a variety of ass. I smiled and dried off.

"You want breakfast?" Lizzie said as I came up the hall.

"Naw, I'll get something on the way home to the shop. Here's your money for your monthly bills."

She came up, kissed me and said, "Again I am sorry for calling her that and I hope you hit me up soon."

"Girl you know I will because your pussy is the best but right now I have to go."

I left out and stopped at McDonald's for breakfast. What the hell wrong with Lizzie, she knows outside of home and restaurants I don't eat. The bitch won't catch me slipping like that.

CHAPTER 3

I arrived at the shop and before getting out, I called Solo.
I needed to hear her voice but I got the voicemail. What the hell
she doing that she can't answer he damn phone? I thought while
I hung up her voicemail.

"I know I don't need to call you every day but this
morning I needed to hear from you. I miss you and it is hard on
me. When you get a chance hit me back up. I love you dearly
bye."

Opening the door of the office was Mudcat. He was
cheesing too hard but I enlighten him anyway by saying,
"What?"

"Where the hell was your ass last night, I hand some
pussy lined up for you."
"Shit, I was fucking off with Lizzie and last night the
pussy was extra creamy and good as hell."

"Damn L. T., don't tell me you falling for her bitch ass?"
Mudcat asked.
"Hell no, I was just saying the pussy was good as hell and
shit, I cream and took my ass to sleep."

"Yo ass stayed the night? Hell naw, you didn't do that
one did you?" Mudcat asked another question.

"Yup ya boy fucked and went to sleep."
"You the one telling me not to stay out and here, yo ass
go doing it."

"My wife was not at home and shit, I was tired as hell after I let go that big ass nut."

"Was it good?"
"Shit, she fucked me with her eyes open and the light on."
We laughed because we know that if you get a bitch to stare as you fuck her, you doing something psychologically to her ass.

"What you do last night?" I asked my friend.
"The usual, fucked a friend or two and got my dick sucked by one and two."
"Yo ass still has energy to come to work?" I asked.
"Hell naw. I worked hard yesterday because I know when those two bitches get on my dick, there is no way I can work and make it good."

We laughed some more before I said, "Right now, I am going to call Solo again."
"You go on and do that. I'm going to change the oil and strainer in the Crown Vic."
I dialed her number again and it went to voicemail. Leaving another message I said, "You ok? I still haven't heard from you. Let me know you ok, babe. I love you."

Soon as I hung up, she called me back and said pleasantly, "Good morning L. T."
"Babe, it's good to hear your voice."
"What's up?" She asked.
"Nothing, I needed to hear your voice that's all."

"Have you eaten your breakfast? You know you get cranky if you don't this early."

"Yeah, I went to McDonald's but I haven't eaten yet."
"Go on and eat, the shop can wait. If you don't eat, you won't do as well as you normally would do."

"Ok. I will try not to call you but I miss the fuck out of you and my body is calling out for some Solo."

She started laughing again and that sound is really music to my ears. Thinking of anything, I asked "Before you go, tell me how you been?"

"Lonely but I'll manage. It's for a good cause."
"Ok. Go on back to whatever it is you were doing."
"Ok. Love you babe."
Faintly I replied, "Love you more babe."
Soon as I was off with her I began to eat my breakfast. Moments later, Mudcat came in and said, "Someone in the shop wants to see you."

"Have them to come in."
Mudcat stepped to the side and Dandy pranced in. Dandy was our go to girl and there were many times, Mudcat and a few more of us would fuck the pussy dry. I don't like sloppy seconds so I always went first. Even though she was a flipper, her pussy was good and the mouth piece wasn't bad either. Along the way, Mudcat wanted more of her so she stopped messing off with him. She said his attitude was horrible but she could deal with it.

However, my attention went back to Dandy. The first things I saw and have always loved are her long slender ballerina legs. Mainly the way her painted toes, has rings on them as she makes her entrance. Wearing a short ass skirt and no panties as usual, her nipples pierced through her small tee shirt and I can't forget the huge ass lips that can suck you dry, if you let her. Damn she looking good and smelling even better. Now I am imagining how her tongue ring feels on my mushroom cap. The only problem isn't her red flaming hair it's her ghetto ass attitude.

"I can tell you like what you see."

"Hell yeah, I like what I see. What the fuck up with you?" I asked as she sat in front of me fanning her legs back and forth.

She knows that I am alert and watching the long pussy mouth of hers as she wiggles. The way her pussy lurks at me, makes me want to it more.

"Can I help you today?" I said as I spoke to her pussy and not her face.
"You need to come over and check the plumbing at the house. It's backed up and not letting anything out."

"You could have called me for that and not come by."

"You mean to miss this fucking opportunity and not see yo ass at yo house, get fucking real. I mean I seldom get a chance to come by when Solo is not here."

"What makes you think she not here?" I asked.

"When your dick gets more free time, you make it your business to find out. Besides if the dick is not with his wife and it's not with me, then where the fuck my dick at if his ass ain't in my ass?"

I laughed because I don't know how she found out that my wife was gone. Then again she always finds out shit that is where I get some information from. This ghetto pussy bitch knows everything.

"I'm still tired from last night."

"Well bring yo ass to check out my plumbing."

"Can't, got to make that money today and it's time for your rent" I said for she is the only one I am fucking that pays rent because she has a man.

"I got you but you have to come to the house to get it" She spoke with a hint of mischievous.

When I finished writing the receipt, Dandy got up and I watched the way she walked off. The swaying of her hips reminded me of the way she suck dick and let you dog fuck her, hell yeah I'm getting that ass. Feeling heated, I thought, *"I do need a pick me up piece this morning."*

Her tall ass leaned forward and touched her toes as her ass hung high in the air. I walked behind her and slid my two fingers off in her gushy pussy. Gently I massaged the fingers in and out of her. She was working her ass and I liked that feel. Deciding to stop right now before I go against my morals and take her in my shop. I do respect my wife and would not fuck in our home, on my job and in her car but the way this ghetto bitch working it, I better quit. Pulling out my two fingers, Dandy turned around and stared at me as she sucked my fingers ever so slow.

"You my freak" I said to her seriously.

"Come on, I have time and you the dick I need this morning. I said I got you."

I put my phone on silent and said to Mudcat, "I'll be back, hold things down for me until I get back. Her plumbing stopped up and I have to go fix it."

Mudcat looked at me and said, "Shit, let me unstop that line."

"Hell naw Nigga, yo ass too small and you can't lay pipe like L. T. I have a big pipe problem, not a child's problem."

"Aight bitch crack ya damn joke, I see."

"I got yo bitch and you can't handle yo bitch, so you try to fuck with this bitch, bitch."

"Don't you get tired of fighting other motherfuckers over yo man?"

"If they keep on trying to take my damn place, hell yeah I'm fighting the bitches. I have to let those bitches know that just because I dance doesn't mean I can't fight."

"Shit that's fucked up. Having to fight every time you look around when you can have a man like me. You won't have that damn drama if you were my bitch" Mudcat said as he smiled at Dandy.

"Nigga yo ass don't have enough money and yo ass can't lay pipe like I need. So what the fuck would I fuck off with yo ass, just to cheat on yo ass?"

Mudcat did not like that fact that Dandy kept throwing up that he can't fuck like she needs him too. *Men don't like other men to hear if they are lacking in the bedroom department and they don't like for other men to know if they don't make that money.* Mudcat spoke with a devilish grin, "You know what? L. T. fuck shit out that big pussy bitch. Make her ass pay."

"Oh, my pussy going to pay alright but too bad you little ass won't be the one making her pay."

The main problem was, his dick was too small for her and she needed a healthy size pipe. Every so often, we would flip her out; not today I'm greedy. However, I love my wife but there is something about having a habit of fucking who you wanted when you wanted. That mentality hasn't changed. Right now, I'm wilding out.

Most of the time would fuck off with Dandy was when Lizzie was out of town; better yet, when Solo ass was tripping. Other than that, I fucked other bitches for their money or for a good guy reputation. I got in my car and followed Dandy. The more I drove, the more I thought about this one bitch that has children. I have taken her and the children to the park.

I haven't tapped her yet but it's in the making. I see the way she watches me. She sees the way I interact with her children. By the way that is not for play, I truly enjoy her children. But women like her, looking for that role model. So far I have been that. I have bought toys, sent her flowers and called just to see how they were doing; for no reason being a gentleman. I know her type and if I play my act right, I will be getting her goods."

Soon as I parked at the house, Dandy went inside. She knows business first. I opened my hand and she counted me out six one hundred dollar bills, I placed it in my wallet as I handed her the receipt I hand written. She took the receipt and laid it on top a pile of mail. The house was clean as usual as she said, "You know my nigga is gone off shore and he won't be back for two weeks."

"I know and I will be taking care of that slack while he is swimming in the middle of nowhere."

"Right now, yo ass ain't taking care of shit. You over there running yo fucking mouth."

Giving her my charming smile, I walked closer to her and pulled off my pants. Sitting back on the couch in a relaxing formation, I placed my legs a part. Dandy got between my legs and began sniffing my dick. Now her acting like a dog and shit is brand new and for her to do that was making me wonder; although, one brush of that tongue and my dick forget all about her dog ass ways.

My toes were spreading and pulling in every direction. The way her neck muscles were going at it, I knew she was trying to throw that mouth piece on me and it was working. She mobbed up and down, kissing the sides and soaking my balls with her spit. I could feel the nut coming up and she knew it so she stopped.

My legs were shaking with anticipation as she kissed the dick head one last time. When she got up, I began to place the condom on and thinking, *"Sounds silly to let her suck the dick bare but put on a condom to fuck. We men do crazy ass shit. But have you ever had your dick sucked with a condom on? That shit doesn't feel as good as bare. I would have fucked her bare but there is no telling who else is fucking her. I know the bitch not faithful because she fucking up on her ole man and me? I'm really not faithful; not to her ghetto ass anyway."*

Dandy's beautiful breast caught my attention as they bounced back like springs to bring my thoughts back to her. With one throw, she was straddling me and easing that nice ass on top of me. Reaching up, I positioned my huge hands under each chocolate mound and squeezed with delight.

She eased down on top of me. I put my hands on each hip while she worked her hips like she does that stripper pole. I could only meet her demands as she would drop her ass on my thighs to say, "Throw that dick! Fucking throw that motherfucker on me!"

A few more bouncing and she got up and rode the dick backwards. The way her firm ass looks as she takes the dick is supreme. Knowing that men go by what we see, I loved the view that was in my eyes and that was making me throw that dick harder and harder. The more that ass bounced and rolled on that dick the more, I continued to throw that dick on her ghetto ass. "Get that nut out!"

Suddenly, she began to go slow and I could feel every ounce of that pussy. I promise I was so deep that I could feel the beginning of her stomach. Instantly, cum filled the condom and she was smashing down on my dick like her pussy was swallowing it up. Fuck no! Her ass has to get up but she continued to prop against me. Finally, I slightly nudged her up and she moved back.

"Go get me a towel. I got to get the fuck back to the shop."

She stared at me and spoke, "Damn, yo ass can't kick it for a few? I did just work yo mother fucking ass out. Give the bitch more than a nut but yo ass wants to run the fuck off. You act like you can't give a bitch a conversation and shit."

"Why the fuck will I hang around and talk? Why the hell would I just kick it, when the point of kicking it is fucking? Shit we already did that. Hell the nut was our conversation. It's time to go about our ways, shit the fucking was damn good and you accomplished that shit. Hell, I have a business to run. I can't make money hanging around this bitch just talking."

Dandy got an attitude. I got up slowly as I held the condom on and went to the bathroom. Once I was over the toilet, I took the condom off and nut splashed into the toilet. I continued to hold the condom over the toilet with my left hand. I took the towel from Dandy and wash my face. I pulled the condom off and allowed it to drip over the toilet.

She soaped the towel up so I could wash my dick. I handed her the towel, and she rinsed the soap off. I got it back and finished cleaning up my dick. After that I wrapped the used condom in the towel. Before I left the bathroom, I do like I always do and that is flushing the toilet.

I flush the toilet to make sure that my nut was gone bye-bye. I always take my nut condom with me because bitches are scandalous. Anytime nut comes in contact with pussy; even just a drop she can get pregnant. Most of them will place that ejaculation from inside the condom, towel in them. Then bam! Take all yo damn money. Not me, no fucking way. I don't plan to get tied up and lose all I worked for on a bitch I'm just fucking. I got too fucking much going on. After I got cleaned up, I left.

Since my wife been gone, I've been fucking left and right. I remember that she used to tell me that pussy will fall at my feet when she was not around. Making me grin, she was right. If Solo was home, Dandy would not have come over. She would have called me; I would have come over. Nevertheless, it was a good ass nut this morning.

Arriving back at the shop, I threw the towel in the thrash. I never thought about my cell until something told me to look at it. When I pulled it out, I saw that my wife's number. Out loud, I hollered out, "Fuck! Solo called."

In haste, I called her back, and she answered, "About time you called me back. I was getting worried."

"Hey babe there's no need to get worried. I didn't hear the phone. What's wrong?"

"I was calling because I wanted to fuck for the last time before I really wait for you."

I could have passed out. I just wasted that nut on Dandy and now my wife wants me to sleep with her. I can't do anything with her but eat that pussy. Being that she calling me, she doesn't want a damn licking, she wants a sticking too. Gathering my thoughts, I calmly stated, "As much as I want the pussy in my face and on my dick, I can't."

"Why is that? Why you can't give it to me?"
Gathering my thoughts, I proclaimed, "You want me to take time and I can't do that if you allow me to enjoy what you have. I need our next sexual union to be filled with an over rated explosive experience. I have to figure out what I need to do and I can't do that if I am making love to you like I deeply need too."

The phone was silent. I didn't know what to think but she broke the silence by saying, "L. T. Thanks so much for passing that little test."

I hand never been so excited in my life. My grandfather always told me that when you fuck in the streets, make sure you can perform at home- you never know what she wants to do when you return. In some cases, the woman will try you, just to see if you can do it. Luckily for me, she is on her "I need time alone adventure." I spoke what Solo wanted to hear.

"What test babe? What are you talking about?"

"I know how much you enjoy my lovemaking, and I enjoy it too but I needed to see if you would obey my wishes or come on anyway."

"What does that prove?"
"It proves to me that you are being considerate of what is happening in our marriage."

"Well I told you if you need space, you can have it. It doesn't mean I approve of it."

"Babe get back to work. I love you."
"I love you too babe."
When I hung up, Mudcat said, "That shit was close wasn't it."
"Hell yeah. There was no way I was going to sleep with my wife after Dandy."

"Was the pussy still good?"
"It was better than good and her mouth was on point."
We bump hands and laughed about that ghetto trick.
"The next time, you can come with me."
"If I didn't have work to do, I would have come to get my dick suck by the ghetto body bitch. I also need to crash is it cool to come to ya place? "
"Shit yeah, you good."
"What about Dandy, now?"

"I said we have to make plans to flip her ass out again before Solo comes home. When she gets back, I have to be as horny as hell."

"Nigga you get pussy on the regular, how you going to do that?"

"Fake it!"

"Shit, these bitches been running you up and down the streets, since Solo been gone."

"They may have me up and down the streets but when I'm in the streets, I'm fucking them."

We laughed and laughed. Mudcat went back to work and I documented the payment from Dandy with a smile. I received a few calls about some iron and scheduled appointments for three suburban's to come through the shop for stripping. One alone is worth up to fifteen thousand dollars depends on the years. Right now, I have three 2010's coming and countless of other vehicles Mudcat is working on. I am looking at some serious ass money to put back and I have to look out for my boy.

CHAPTER 4

I went to bed tired as hell. It hadn't been a long time since I fucked back-to-back like that without fucking Solo but it opened my eyes were the saying of OG Pete, *"These streets were here before you were born, and they will be here when you die; you can't beat those streets."*

I checked the clock at it was three am. I thought, *"That's the usual time old people say spirits talk to you, go figures."*

Deciding to get a glass of running water, I went to the kitchen and heard a noise. Walking slowly towards the living room, I picked up the iron club. Once I came around the corner, I was about to swing but I heard, "Don't hit me! Don't hit me!"

It was Mudcat's voice. I questioned quickly, "Man what the hell you doing in here?"

"You forgot I told you that I was going to stay for a few days."

"Hell yeah, I forgot. I almost put your brains on the damn floor of this Persian rug."

"Hell yeah, you were that is why I started screaming."
We began to laugh.
"Now my ass woke."
"You want something to drink?"
"Naw man you know I'm an occasional drinker and this is not an occasion. Knock yourself out."

"You don't have to tell me twice."

Mudcat went to the fridge and opened up a can of Bud Light. I fixed a ham sandwich and got some water. We sat at the kitchen table and began talking.

"Man, you always drinking water or something. As long as I have known you, liquor and wine has not been your taste."

"Mudcat, I grew up where drinking is the last thing you do. It's about getting on the grind and getting that damn money."

"But yo ass has a nice house, a wonderful undercover operation, a gorgeous wife and plenty of pussy on the side. Why you not happy, I mean Solo is perfect?"

"Yes she is perfect to some degree. A man like me doesn't have time to be as happy as one can if he is focused on that green paper. You don't want to get too comfortable then get broke because that shit will happen so quick your head could spin."

"Motherfucker you have cash on top of cash. What mo yo ass want?"

"So do you but my thing is, I don't want to do this all my life. I eventually want to have children and when you have children, there is their college education, clothes, accidents; which, makes doctor bills and expenditures that surpasses all what I have stored up. I don't want my family to ask for shit."

"That's one thing I can say and that is yo ass be on top of that paper."

"Got to, if I don't do it another mother fucker will."

My friend and I talked a few more minutes. We actually reminisced about all the pussy we have plotted on and got. I had no idea that there were that many women I slept with before my wife and after my wife, mainly two. I went back to bed and went to sleep; this time with the future heavily on my mind.

The next morning, I was refreshed to make more money. Quickly I showered and put on a matching outfit. Going downstairs, I noticed that Mudcat was up for the day. However, today is Saturday and that meant we have work to do because this is one of our busiest days.

Mudcat may have eight to nine cars to strip; while, I do some custom painting. You wouldn't think of all the white people that comes to my shop for custom this or custom that. I love fooling with them because they make sure they pay. We have been at it all day in the shop, and my cell phone hasn't stopped ringing. It's been Lizzie and Dandy all day long; wanting to know if I can fuck.

I don't know what the hell is going on but neither one of them is my wife; come to think of it. I may need to check them both again. The more I thought about Solo the more intense my paintings on the cars became. Everyone that saw their new painted whip fell in love with it from the door. Then I stepped back and checked the painting out, the more I liked the new created way my designs were.

I've been working like a damn slave with painting and taking vehicles a part. I didn't realize how I have been working without coming up for air. I decided to go into the office and sit my ass down. I picked up a bottle of water and began drinking it. For the first time since I fucked back-to-back like that, pussy hand been the last thing on my mind and to be honest, fuck pussy; I need to make this money. Soon as that thought came across me, my shop phone rang. I looked at the caller ID and it was Solo, my wife. Snatching up the phone, I spoke, "Hey babe what's up?"

"I love you, but I don't love your lifestyle anymore."

She startled me and I don't know where all this was coming from. I continued to listen to her speak, "I have my ideas of you and your affairs with other women but them calling my phone has gone too damn far!"

"What? Who is calling your phone? Saying what? Who are you talking about?"

She did not say a word. I assumed she was waiting on me to shut up and so I did and she said through the mountain of tears, "I don't know who she is but she keeps calling my job saying I better stay away from you. You my husband! Who the hell she thinks she is? Then she spoke that you belong to her and not me."

"Babe, you don't believe that shit do you?"

"Right now, I don't know what to believe."

"What you mean, you don't know what to believe? I love you and I am here working my ass off to make that damn money for our future."

"I know you are at the shop now and from the way they talk, you spend your nights there."

"No the hell I don't. When did they call you? What's the damn number?" I questioned.

"It doesn't matter. Either I believe you or I don't."

"True. You should believe I love you with everything I have."

She paused for a few more moments and said, "It is not your love for me that is in question. It's the other women that you trick off with."

"Do you believe me? Do you believe that I don't love you?"

"It is not about your love for me. It is about you being faithful to me!"

"Don't make shit out to be more than it is. You said yourself that the devil wants us broken up and shit. Hell he doing a good ass job with you living over there and I am living here alone. Don't you think he wants to play mind games on us? You act like I don't have ideas about you fucking another motherfucker."

"Me! Fucking up on you! You a damn lie! How can I be calm and you just said you think about me fucking."

To sound very convincing, I began to make my voice tremble and crack as I spoke, "I didn't say you were fucking. I said don't you think the devil plays with my mind too about you? You fine and have a lot going for you. You smart and you are so much fun to be around. Now me, I'm the one that's not about shit. I grew up hustling and that is all I know. Yeah, I am handy with my hands but shit what the fuck is that if they can't hold the love of my life with them? I might as well be worthless of a man that can't keep his wife at home. Shit I can't keep you happy. Now look at us? I'm alone and on top of that bullshit trying to mess what we have going up."

I waited to see if she bought what I just sold her. A majority of it was from the heart but parts of it were bullshit covered up sweetly. Moments later she spoke, "Don't say that. You are more than that and if you don't think so, I love you. I am happy to be your wife, and you are a wonderful husband. I do rely on the old saying you know, where there is smoke there is a fire. It could be something innocent as they want your money or want to take my place because I appear to have it all. I don't know. It could be you are really doing all this and making me be dumb to what is going on. I want to believe you with my heart. I honestly do but right now, it's just best that we continue to stay as we are."

"I listen to your talks about that church shit and how the devil wants us a part. I listen and I take it all in. Babe, you have to know I love you and you my life; you everything to me. I give you anything you need all you have to do is ask and the shit's yours. Don't do this to me, I need you. I promise I need you. Above all, I need to know you believe me. I can't take it if you don't believe me."

"I believe you; even though, I have doubts. I can't help but have doubts because we both know that when a man makes money there are women standing around trying to get a little bit of it."

"I'm going to find out who the hell is lying on me. I've been here all day with Mudcat working like a slave."

"I know I called your cell, and you didn't answer. I presumed you were in the office or doing some painting."

"I love you Solo, and I can't wait to see that smile on your face again. I detest so when you are not happy."

"I love you too babe and I can't wait to be home with you again. Goodbye."

"Don't say goodbye, say I'll see you later."

She chuckled and spoke sweetly, "Ok. I will see you later. I love you."

"I love you more Solo, I love you more."

After Solo and I hung up, my mind began racing. I need to figure out who is telling my wife all this shit on me. This is the second time and the last damn time, somebody runs their mouth about L. T. Times. Whoever it is, does not understand when you play with my life especially when Solo is involved; the shit gets personal. I decided to call Lizzie up and see her tonight. I have something on my mind and I'm not street smart for nothing. The phone rung once and on the dime, she picked up. I asked, "Can we meet up tonight babe?"

"You know you can. Are you coming over here?"

"We will go to a hotel tonight. I want to take you out and have desert later, if that is ok."

"Yes, it is you know I love going out with you in public."

"I know you do too and since I am alone more, I intend to do that more often."

"What time you coming by to pick me up?"

"I will be there in another hour or so. I have to finish up here at the shop, make reservations and get the hotel room."

"I know I'm your number one outside girl."

"You my girl period and it is time I treat you as such. So wear something sexy- something that will keep my mind off eating the food."

She began to laugh as I hung up. I dialed Dandy's number. Just like Lizzie, she picked up just like that, "What's up sexy?"

"My motherfucking legs again but this time put them bitches around your neck. You don't ever eat my pussy, but I suck yo dick like it ain't shit. What's that about?"

I began to laugh because Dandy always makes me laugh. She has not failed me yet by her roughneck bitch ass attitude and being straight to the point. Stating to her I spoke, "You sleeping with more than just me, that's what it is."

"Damn you fucking what's her name."

"Solo."

"Hell yeah you fucking her ass and who ass else, that will give you the guts."

"The only ass you need to worry about is me fucking you. Solo is my damn wife and hell yeah, I'm going to fuck her. You know that."

"I'm just checking to see if yo ass gone call out some other bitch name."

Dandy is like other women. They know they aren't the only ones so they try to trip you up to see if you would ever tell on yourself. Most of all it is just the way she talks, and it is stupid as hell but her pussy and her mouth makes up for what she lacks. I began to laugh as I said, "I want to take my favorite girl out this Monday. I haven't been showing you love because I have been busy and shit. I care about you Dandy, and I should express myself clearly to you."

"Damn babe, this pussy must have showed the fuck out to make you want to take my ass out. You know how fucking long it has been since we been out together?"

"I know that is why I am calling. I need you to know that we want you more in my life than you are."

"Who the fuck is we?"

"Me and my dick."

"What the fuck ever?" Dandy exploded.

I see she needs more proof that I am for real about her so I said, "I intend to make you my number one girl. Fuck the rest of those bitches. You keep it real, you don't lie to me and you have been here for me. Honestly, your ghetto ass pussy is the best."

She waited for a few minutes before saying, "Yo ass lying. You still with yo wife."

"That ain't got shit to do with it. I am still with her but hell that is for business purposes. What do you say about me taking yo ass out, and spending a little of your money on you?"

"Yo ass knows I have to fucking work. I can't go no damn where but to the club and dance my ass off."

"How about if I come to the club and spend those dollars on you?"

Very loudly she proclaimed, "Hell no. Yo ass may trip and shit if another mother fucker wants my time. You may start trouble. I don't come to your place, and cut the fuck up. So I don't need you coming to mine doing the same damn thing."

Laughing inward, I wanted to hang up on this chick. There was no damn way I would get angry over a trick that anybody can fuck. But to make her think I am all into her, I would put on a show just for her. I see now this bitch doesn't think she is important enough to me. I'm going have to put some authority in my tone just for her. Taking a sigh I spoke, "Babe listen, yo ass is mine and as long as they don't be grabbing your breast and you making the lap dance too damn good; I'll be good but if it goes to damn far, I'm going to say something."

"See, yo ass don't need to come and ain't no fucking telling how things will jump off. I can't afford to have yo ass coming here and fucking up my damn job and shit."

"Your ass is my damn woman; fuck that mother fucker on the water. That is my pussy and if I want to come see my pussy, guess what the fuck I am going to do; come see my pussy!"

"Listen here L. T. yo ass wife name is Solo not Dandy, get the fucking names right."

"You need me! Who else is going to feed your hungry ass? Me. Who is going to make sure you have money lined up, when he doesn't want to help take care of you? Me. So I don't want to hear what you yapping about and don't breathe my damn wife's name again out your mouth."

"Shit. L. T. it's not like I get all yo mother fucking money. Hell, I still pay rent but those other bitches don't. I'm the damn one that tricks off, get that money and break you off some."

"Those other women don't have dick coming in and out shit I let them live in, you do. So again, shut the fuck up. I will be coming by your damn job and if I don't fucking like the way those mother fuckers touches you, I will shut that motherfucker down. That way, I'll be giving you the entire dick you need. Is that understood?"

"Damn babe. Yeah, I get it. Shit you acting like that and shit, hell yeah you my number one Nigga. Come to the club and I will dance just for you."

"Ok. I see you Monday and stay sweet for me."
I got off the phone with her. I was going to say that I could not believe she bought those lies but I am who I am. A slight knock was at the door, "Come in."

It was Mudcat. He appeared tired as I said, "Man take a break."

"I am. I saw you taking a break and I hand to stop for myself."
"Man, you not on a white man's clock."
He looked at me and asked, "What you got going on for tonight?"
"I'm going out tonight."
"That's what's up."
"Hell yeah, got to take Lizzie out and make her feel important in my life."
"I don't know how you do it. I don't know how you have all these bitches under control, and they don't once act up or step the fuck out of line."

"It's not about controlling them. It's about you being the man. I'm quite sure they may have heard about someone else, but they all know that I have a wife. They know that when they see Solo and I out; they better not come to me about anything. If they have a complaint they better call during operation hours."

Before we could talk more, the office phone rung and I was surprised. I glanced up Mudcat and he spoke silently, "Who is that?"

I lifted my finger for him to be quiet as I put the phone on speaker. The caller said, "Hi may I please speak to Mr. Times?"

"Hi this is he. May I ask who is calling?"
"It's me Monica, Monica Craft."

Mudcat mumbled with his lips, "She sounds sexy as hell!"

I smiled because he has never seen her in person, and he was not lying about her looks. Returning back to the conversation, I spoke, "What a pleasant surprise. How are you doing?"

"I was calling you to ask if you have any more rental properties available."

"I sure do. What is your price range?"

She was quiet. I pretended that we lost some type of service by asking, "Hello you there?"

"Yes, I am here."

"What is your price range?" I asked her again.

This time, I spoke first by saying, "I tell you what, I will show you what I have available along with their prices. You then tell me what you might possibly be looking for and what you may able to afford."

"That sounds great to me. When can we meet?" Monica asked with joy.

"Are you busy now? I mean if I can't come now, it will be another three to four days before I am able to show you."

"Tonight sounds perfect."

"Ok. I will be over in a few."

"Ok. See you then."

Soon as we hung up, Mudcat said, "Who the hell is that?"

"That's Monica. You don't remember me telling you about her?"

"No, I can't remember. Shit you tell me about too many bitches as is. Refresh my memory."

"She is the one with a short hair that cups her oval brown face, about five feet tall, chubby and with four kids under the age of six."

"It still does not ring a bell" Mudcat said.

"The one in the process of a divorce."

"Still don't remember" I asked Mudcat.

"No."

"The one I used to go see and buy shit for when Solo saw the flowers she thought they were for her and I had to give them to her."

"Oh hell yeah! Now I remember."

"Look at this picture of her."

Opening up my phone, I showed him a picture of her. In this picture, she wore a church dress and the kids were not with her. My boy glanced up at me to say, "Damn, you didn't tell me she goes to church. I bet her pussy is good and tight."

"Shit, I don't fuck off with whores all the time. A majority of my bitches have class but this one, she the type that you have to be careful with. Her ass will fall in fucking love."

"Why you fucking off with her then if you know she will fall for the game you spitting?" Mudcat asked.

"I never met a horse I couldn't ride and the harder the chase the better the kill."

He laughed and then I said, "Bitches like her will be faithful to me and she has kids so she's not so much into casual sex or boyfriends here and there. In fact, I got a chance to get around her and her children by being where they were, like parks, McDonald's, and shit like that. Women like that need stability and all that shit."

"How the fuck you find the time to scout this bitch out and how yo ass going to offer her that shit and yo ass got a wife?"

"When you want a woman, you make the time. You let her know that you may be busy, but you are never too busy to spend time with her and her children. As for the stability and shit, by being kind, sweet and good to the children, yeah use the kids to my benefit. The love I show to them is genuine, but I need her to see what a great guy I am that loves spending time with her kids and buying them stuff."

"I like that method."

"It's real and it's something the real father's won't do or doesn't do. By doing this, she falls for me, the entire time but I won't rush her because she has trust issues, so I wait until she comes at me."

"That shit sounds like it will work."

"Man, I've been in the game of gaming women for so long that I know a lot about them just by looking at them, even touching their hand or how they walk. Studying women is like art, like a job and over the years you prefect it."

"You have some pretty ass bitches. Where you find them at?"

I only laughed for I will not tell him all my secrets on where to find my women at. I glanced at the time and said, "Here is the extra doe for the work you did on last week."

Mudcat looked down at the money and said, "That's the shit I'm talking about. I might take one of my hoes out."

"You have just as many women as I do, so who you going to take?"

"Might just pick up a female from the club and treat her ass nice."

"Shit. Do that, increase your bitch list. I have."

We laughed and Mudcat said before leaving out the office, "I'm going to be at yo crib tonight so don't try hitting my ass with that iron rod. I might have a bitch with me."

"Just don't fuck in my bed. I'm the only one that does that."

"How Solo doing?" Mudcat asked.

"Her ass good now but somebody called her phone saying I'm fucking up but she alright."

Mudcat agreed by saying, "That's what's up. Keep them freelance whore's in check."

When he left out, I called Lizzie and told her that I would be late because something came up and I have to go make that money. She understood because she knows I only cancel for Solo and money. Anyway the longer I make her wait, the quicker I make her cum.

Now rocking back in my chair, I placed my feet upon my desk and began to wonder, how the hell somebody is telling my wife shit about me? I am doing the shit she is accusing me of but that is irrelevant. So far to my knowledge she doesn't have any actual proof but I know my wife. She will try to let me hang myself but that is where she is wrong. I haven't gotten this far by being a damn dick led fool. I know when to fuck up and how far to go but it is the women that have their priorities wrong.

They think if they accuse a man of something he would eventually confess but hell no. A real dog ass Nigga not telling shit on his self. He will let you continue to believe what the fuck ever you want; only weak bastards tell. Real men would play her game, continue to lie and manipulate her and women like her for as long as he can. He can live a replica life of pretense just to score brownie points. However, my wife is no spring chicken. That bitch knows shit about the game and how it is played, so I have to keep a step in front of her; so far it has worked.

Now the single bitches that are still on my nuts try to play hard but Niggas like me would wear their ass down like brake pads and then change it on them. Women don't get it that broke ass Niggas don't have anything going for them but sex. That is the only thing they have and if they fuck just right, that is all they need. The bitch will provide a place to stay, food, clothes, her ride, her money and access to everything she has but only if you fuck good or eat pussy better.

Suddenly as I rocked, I heard OG Pete's voice, *"You can't see the picture if you still in it boy."*

I nearly fell over as I heard the saying. I immediately stopped rocking and froze. It was like a light came on and showed me the way. It was if, I understood why Solo left me. Honestly, hearing it from my grandfather makes more sense than her telling me. In fact, how could she see what I am doing if she is still with me? She has to remove herself from my life just to get a glimpse of what is actually going on in my life. Solo is trying to see if she can trust me and if I have been lying to her.

With a new outlook, I went in the house, got dressed and left for Monica's.

CHAPTER 5

I drove for almost an hour to the other side of town. The atmosphere is different. The neighborhood is half white and there are parks almost every corner. It is a young children environment and it felt nice. It felt like the kind of place, I wish I grew up in but didn't. Taking my surroundings in more, you could tell by the stores on the street and way the houses all look that it is absolutely family friendly. When I arrived to Monica's house, she came outside, looking good. If I wasn't married to Solo, she would be my wife because she has morals and she talk about doing better.

Just listening to her would make you want to be that man a woman like her needs, but I am a damn dog. *I can't be faithful to my wife, I'm too far gone I thought as I thought about Monica and how she reminds me so much of my wife.* They talk about the same shit. That is one of the reasons why I admire that in Monica, the second is she has children and is trying to take care of them the best she cans. However, that is where I come in at to trick her ass. I'm not after her heart. I have mine in my chest.

I placed my phone on silent and got out the car. Monica and I hugged. Damn her short ass smells inviting. I don't know how the hell I am to contain myself if she smells like this. Besides my wife knows so fuck it, I'm about to wild the fuck out now fo sho. Anyway, I spoke with a charming smile, "You smell extremely good this evening."

"Thank you and you look nice yourself."

"Thank you. Where are the children?"

She paused and I could tell that something was wrong. Being who I am, I am going to use this to my benefit. Lifting her chin up I asked softly, "Monica what is wrong? Why you seem so sad and broken?"

She leaned closer to me and cried. Me, the gentleman that I am, held her then rocked her soft body to say, "Whatever it is, I am here for you? It's going to be ok. I may not be much of a help but I am your friend. I will do anything to help you and your family. Now where are the children anyway?"

She pulled back from me. When she glanced up, I had never seen such beautiful eyes on a dark skinned woman before. For some reason I was overwhelmed with compassion for her.

"That means so much to me to hear that you are here for me. No man I had ever met wanted to be here for me and here you are. Thank you."

"You are welcome."

I could have let her go but she felt so right in my arms. I loved the idea of being a pretend family man to her right now. Therefore, I continue holding her as she spoke, "They are with their aunt for the weekend because I need to find a place to stay."

"What is wrong with this place?"
"Nothing. This place is perfect, but I have to move out because I don't have the funds to buy my husband out of it. He says we can bypass the legal part of the house, being that the children and I still reside here. Basically, he doesn't have a

lawyer yet. The sad part is he wants his money, more than he wants his children to have a place to call home. "

"What about the kids?" I just had to ask.

"I guess he does not care but they don't know that we have to move because of him."

"Does he pay child support or something?"

"He does but if I pay him out the house, I get half the money back because it will go towards the money he owes. Before I put money in his pocket I would rather move and let the lawyers settle it."

I got a crazy idea and decided to run it by her. I asked, "How about I buy the house from you and give it back to you for free because of the kids."

She looked at me with a puzzled manner and spoke, "Are you serious? I never thought about it."

"Yeah it should work only if you sell the house before you put it in the divorce papers. If not, you will have to sell the house for the rightful value of it. But if you sell now before any paperwork his ass will get five dollars, a dollar for each one of you that he left and tried to make homeless."

"Let me call my lawyer and see what she says."

Monica went back in the house and about twenty minutes later she came back. I was still standing outside the car as she walked up to me and kissed me. I never was kissed like that before. There was an appeal in the way she kissed me in fact she kissed me like a woman in love. Pulling away from her embrace I spoke, "I guess it will work."

She looked up at me and said, "Will it work? It will more than work, my lawyer said it is a great idea. He doesn't have any paperwork, but I have to act fast. She will have the paperwork ready for you to sign."

"That is good for you."
"How can I repay you for helping me?"

Pussy crossed my mind but with her I had to play like a good Nigga and that is be kind. I spoke, "Just take care of the children and let me take you out sometime. I don't mind. You are a great person and I can be your friend."

"Is that all? I mean you spend your money on us and you are a great guy."

My mind was screaming, give me that sweet smelling pussy, and give it to me now! But out of my mouth she heard, "I try to be a good guy but now a days people take misuse the good guy."

Monica took me by the hand and begun to direct me in her direction. Her palms were moist yet soft, as if she was nervous. I knew what she had in mind but I held on. The closer we got to her front door I began to play dumb as I asked, "What are you doing?"

She opened up the front door and didn't look back while she stated, "Just be quiet and let me do this before I lose my nerve."

Once inside we faced stairs as she locked the door. Before she could dim the lights behind us, I saw that it was nice and comfy. To the right, there was a small cozy fire in the fireplace and a blanket nearby and to the left a nice sizeable kitchen. I took inventory that the home reminded me of the home I never had as a child. I continued looking around and I did not see her because I was infatuated with the home and what a home like this represented.

It was the kind of home that you could actually feel love and inviting. Being that I was not from a raised and nurturing environment, I asserted myself in the father position. For right now, I would make believe that this is my wife and those are my children with her. I must have been in another world because she came out of the living room wearing a two-piece black leather biker girl outfit. It only had the bra piece and the leather panties.

"Damn! This bitch likes to role play and I hate role playing but I will be the bike that she takes for a ride tonight."

"You look amazing" I spoke slower as she came closer because she was indeed amazing. The way the clothes clung to her made the anticipated ride worth looking for.

She does not have the body like my other women, but she has the homely personality and suave of innocence that makes up for her body not being what I'm used to. Monica with ease placed her hands on top of mine and gently guided them along her short, curvy body. She stared down into my face for a reaction as she uttered out, "How do I feel?"

She felt like waves in a damn pond that ripples but I smiled and asked, "Are you sure? I mean I don't want you to feel like you owe me because you don't. But touching you like this makes me feel like a child on Christmas morning."

She smiled and spoke tauntingly, "I'm a grown woman and I know when a man wants a woman or when a woman wants a man and I for one want the touch of you, right now. This is a feeling that I have been knocking and now seems to be the right time."

I didn't know how to answer her because she might expect me to stay the night, and I try not to make that a habit with any woman. I also have Lizzie in a couple of hours, so I have to make this nut short. Politely I said again before I fucked her, "Are you sure? I mean really- really sure? I don't want you to cry and shit after you finish fucking off with me. I don't want you to do anything you don't want to do."

She stepped back and began to strip tease for me. When her top came off then her bottom piece, I knew then that she was serious and so was my manhood.

"Sit back and enjoy the show."
I wanted to tell her fuck the show, let me pound that short ass that I been waiting so long to get. But the having to be the nice guy, again I obeyed her and sat back. Monica was not hard on the eyes but my dick doesn't have eyes it only have feelings and right now it is feeling Monica.

The more she undressed the more my dick respected her. I didn't in a way respect her because she is about to fuck a married man like countless of other bitches, regardless of how good of a guy I am, I still belong to another woman. Recovering my thoughts was the command of Monica's body beneath my hands. She spoke softly and tauntingly, "I plan to make you mines tonight."

I could only say, "I belong to you at this moment."

She moved back and allowed me space to get up. I stood up and towered down over her. She gazed at me with her eyes that whispered, "Be gentle." At that moment, I lifted her up to my level as our eyes were locked. I knew that once I enter her, there will be no turning back.

Easily I kissed her with urgency as I placed her body on the thick plushy blanket. This moment was like a scene in a book but it is the one I had only heard of. Monica was in fact the shortest and smallest woman I have ever fucked off and this is going to be fun.

I created trails of kisses all over her top. I slowly took my time and teased each one of her breast. Her moans were exciting but it was the fact that I was finally getting my reward for buying gifts and shit. She was my willing participate as I kissed and kissed her. The time was winding down and I could not continue to hold it. *I hope she don't think I am going to eat her pussy because if she does she is mistaken.*

With further ado, her fat thighs, opened to let me fall deep between her legs. I held up some because she is half my body length and was actually at the middle of my chest. *Fuck this is different* I thought as I positioned my dick to enter her. She licked her lips and closed her eyes. I kept mines open and watched a small frown come across her brow as I entered her tight short pussy.

Slowly I began to work my magic and slower her short ass was throwing her pussy to me. Never had I imagined that I would be fucking this early in the game but, I don't ever underestimate the power of persuasion. Turning my focus back to the piece of ass I was getting, I began to dig into her pussy; as she her legs wrapped around my back. *Being short has its perks* I thought as I was enjoying this pussy.

Monica only let out soft moans as I was working my ass and body muscles on her. The harder I dung into her the more she held onto me. Purposely I fucked her like a bitch. She didn't mind the beating because she was scratching me and leaving her sweat all over me. It was a sloppy good fuck. To be short as she is, she knew how to hold her legs and pull a Nigga deep. To me, I simply appeared to be doing push-ups with my dick.

The more I fucked her the more she laid her short ass there, letting me gig and jog in her. I didn't mind if she didn't mind so I let it be by continuing to lay this pipe to her ass as my sweat dripped onto the top of her hair.
"I can't take it, L. T., this dick good."

"Shush and shoot that nut."

Fuck her nut. I told her to get it but shit. Soon as those words left my mouth, I began moving faster and faster. Monica began moving just as fast and her rhythm was that of a pro. I can't lie, the pussy was making me drown and I love it when the woman thinks I am losing the battle.

With a few more fast strokes, I began to feel dizzy and she began to muffle out tender cries. I knew it was of joy because she hasn't had sex in almost eight months. When my body stopped releasing, I eased off her and saw her hands go up to her face. *What the hell wrong with her?* I thought as I watched the rise and fall of her breast.

"L. T. that was a wonderful feeling you have given me. It has been a very long time since I gave myself to a man. I have been busy to trying to raise my children up and preoccupied with being a role model to them. I had no idea how wonderful that having a man take me like you did would be."

It is at this point that a man has to make the woman feel like he understands what she is saying and be there for her. Pulling her close to me I replied, "I equally feel the same. I am always at my shop trying to make money and keep things afloat and sometimes I lose focus on what is real and what is not. There are days I need a break but don't take one."

"I never intended for this to happen." Monica spoke as she lifted her body up to look at me.

"I don't have regrets. This is the first time, I had an affair."

She was quiet then said, "Was it worth it?"

"Yes, I have never had a short woman before any woman for that matter that takes the way I grind her. I had never experienced a nut like that before."

Monica smiled and said, "Where we go from here?"

"I don't know but I hope you don't expect me to be faithful because I can't."

"I know. Will I see you again?"

I smiled at her because I know that I am the only one tapping her ass and it's good I spoke with my dick, "Yes, you will see me again and I hope we can take the children to the park for your baby boy's birthday coming up."

She spoke with her heart as she stammered, "I didn't think you remembered."
"Why wouldn't I remember? You are the only woman I see when I am with you."

Monica smiled but I was telling her the truth in so many ways. When I am with her I only see her, when I am with Dandy, Lizzie or my wife I only see them. Playing on her trust I spoke, "I am overjoyed you allowed me to be the first man outside your husband to take you. It means a lot to me that you don't trust men, yet you entrusted me with your body."

"L. T. it takes me time before I can sleep with a man. It is something about you that makes me want you. Do you know how long I have waited for you?"

"No how long?" I spoke as I saw the time behind her on the clock.

"Since the first day you fixed my car battery at the store and told me you own a body shop. I had never wanted to rush into bed with any man. The sex tonight is indescribable and like no other. Let's go shower."

Before she reached for my hand my mind was going crazy. *I know damn well this bitch isn't in love after fucking one time?* I thought as I waited on her to guide me. She then said, "I'm happy I waited for a man like you to take me. It was worth the wait. Don't you agree?"

All I wanted to do was nod yes because I did not trust my mouth to speak. If it did, it would probably ruin this moment for her; then again, fuck her moment. Thinking, *I better hold off before I fuck her moment up, if I want this piece of ass that no one is getting but me.*

"I can't understand a nod."

"You were worth the waiting, and I hope this is a happy memory for you."

"It is, L. T. and no matter how things turn out, I will not forget you."

Smiling I was thinking, *if she really knew how much of a dog ass I really am, she will forget me and everything pertaining to me. Then I remembered what OG Pete always said, "If you going to break a woman's heart and you don't want her to forget you on any level, don't just be replaceable be hard to replace."*

The giggling of her buns in my sight broke up my thoughts about OG Pete's sayings because to be short, her ass knows how to get a man's attention. Watching her short cheeks wobbled up and down turned me on, again.

"What the hell is going on? She turned around and looked at me to say, "I feel you getting aroused."

"What makes you say that?"

Giggling she responded, "My ass told me so."

This woman was right, my dick was thinking, and I didn't want him to think; as I followed behind her. It usually takes me about three nuts per fuck session, and I need to save the last two for Lizzie. I don't need to give Monica syrupy ass any more ideas but shit what the hell, let me indulge in this second.

We went upstairs to shower together. I was actually enjoying this lie; for Monica is fun to be with. Bath time with her will be forever in my mind because it was my first time acting like this with any woman. She would turn around for me to wash her short ass back, in return she washed mine. The touching of course leads to sexual water fights in the big shower; which also leads to stimulating a sexual position.

I faced Monica as the water dripped down on her face. She looked up at me and asked, "What? What is it?"

"You are perfect as well as beautiful."

"You just saying that."

"I can say a lot of things, and I will say a lot of things but remember you are far more beautiful than any woman I have ever been with."

"Even though, I am short with four children?"

"That doesn't have anything to do with it. Actually, it is what makes you perfect."

I leaned into her face and kissed her. Monica reached up and brought her arms around my neck. I didn't want to break up the kissing, but she was too short for me to hold up and kiss at the same time. *I be damned if I hurt my back for her short ass* thinking such as I did, I let her kisses go and picked her up. At this point, I placed the woman's back against the cool, wet bathroom tile. I needed her weight against the wall and not on me.

She held onto my waist with her legs and eased her onto my throbbing third leg. The moment our genital areas connected it was like lightening striking. My knees buckled and I almost dropped her on her ass in the shower; luckily my hands are on her hips. She chuckled a bit but I didn't see shit funny. I began pinning her against the wall and grinding her as if I were squeezing water out of a towel. In my mind, Monica was my wife and how this is our first time fucking since she left. *Damn this is kitty-katt is just right* I thought as I rolled my dick around in half circles to make my muscles flex.

I looked down at her, and her eyes were closed. I slightly smiled because one of my many rules is: you don't ever close your eyes when you're fucking because then you're making love. I only make real love to my wife. *Silly bitch! I screamed in my mind, I do not love you; only these guts you give.*

Women like Monica have to be fucked slowly and if you leave her alone, you must back away just as slow. Any sudden movement could overthrow what has been done and right now, if she wants to let this married man fuck her, then fuck it. I will fuck the shit out of her mind, heart and life up. She is good but not good as a nut. I continued on my journey of fucking her short ass.

The more I pounded on her, the more, she only moaned. I began to test the waters with her by banging her on the shower background a little harder. She did not open her eyes. I then began shoving her heavily on my dick as I stomped with each thrust; still no movement. However, on this day she was trying to throw it back to me but it was a slow fight. I was putting this pipe to her ass and working her out in this shower. It is funny how she was just letting me do it, how she was letting me put her ass through the ringer. The more she allowed me the more I literally fucked her.

Not giving a damn that she will be sore or can't walk after I let her go was not of my concern. My only plan is to fuck her good and drop her ass like a bad habit. During this time, her hefty ass became heavy as hell. The reason is, I shot nut all inside her and she in return almost squeezed the shit out of my hips for her orgasm. Quickly as I can, I released her. *Fuck straining my arms for her short, heavy ass.*

When Monica's feet came in contact with the shower floor, she fell on me. Gasping for breath she retorted, "Damn L. T. I have never been fucked like this before in my life! Damn Nigga shit!"

Being a gentleman in her eyes, I placed a kiss on her forehead and turned back to face the water. I needed to shower up and try to make my way of escape. Monica finished her shower as well and let me in the bathroom alone. Honestly, she is perfect for someone else and I can't help it if she is just life in the streets to me.

Smiling I got out the shower and dried off. I remembered I just had sex bare. What the hell was I thinking? I couldn't change it and the only excuse I have for myself is I got caught up but never again.

CHAPTER 6

Wrapping a towel around me, I went downstairs and did not see Monica. I went in the living room where my clothes were. I heard her hollering, "You getting dressed!"

"Yeah" I hollered back.

"I will be out in a minute, I'm in the kitchen."

"Yeah, I'm going to make a call."

Monica walked from the kitchen soon as I picked up the phone to dial Lizzie.

"I'm not going to make it this evening and will have to postpone."

"What?" Lizzie stated with a hint of disappointment.

"I said I am not going to make it this evening and will have to postpone."

"You with someone else, aren't you?" Lizzie asked.

"I am with someone and we are discussing matters."

"L. T., don't tell me you standing me up and its' not for your wife!"

"You need to change your tone?" I spoke with warning.

The phone was silent for a second then she said, "What you want me to do, I'm here?"

"I'll tell Mudcat to go pay another night for me. That way if I get a chance to come by and see what you are talking about also you will be there."

"Ok. I'm sorry I just assumed you were with another woman."

"That is not your place to do anything. That is on my end."

"You right."

"Later."

Monica stood there with sandwiches and sodas. I held up one finger for her to wait a minute as I picked up the phone and called Mudcat. Each and every time I call him and I don't say anything for a minute that means you are on speaker phone, and he knows the code. At this point we set up the woman so she will believe more of what is said to her.

"Man, I need you to go by and pay another night for Ms. Lizzie. She is going to stay there until I can get by and see what she is talking about."

"Which hotel?"

"I put her up in the Marriot."

"Alight, need anything else?"

Looking over at Monica I spoke, "I may come in late tonight because I am with a special woman, and she means something to me."

"Man, you sound cheerful. I'm happy you're not pouting here over Solo. She left you because she doesn't want the fine things in life and she'll be alright when realizes you have found someone else special."

Monica is smiling hard and from her it is genuine. I smiled back and even blew her a kiss to sweeten the deal.

"Well let me get off the phone. She just came in and I want to spend my time with her and not talking to you. Tell Ms. Lizzie that I will see her as soon as I can and thank you for helping me out."

"Anytime."

I hung up and Monica placed the food tray on the coffee table as she sat beside me to say with sympathy, "Wow, I had no idea that your wife left you."

"Yeah, she did."

In a fast haste, I spoke, "You are not a rebound and the pussy; girl you put it on me. I have wanted you too much to turn you down. It's just that I have a lot going on."

"You getting a divorce?"
I looked at this bitch. I'm not leaving my wife for no damn body if I can help it. When I am in the streets, I am street

and when I am with my wife I am at home. Right now I fuck these streets ever damn day I can and if these tricks and bitches want me to fuck them too, fine join the damn club.

Pretending to be hurt as I spoke, "I don't know. We haven't really talked since she been gone and I'm lonely and don't know what to do. I have money and shit but that doesn't make me happy. I want to be loved when I come home and it's not there. I spend every dime I get to provide a comfortable place for her and I'm always at the shop by the house. It's like nothing I ever do is good enough for her and yet all I do is for her. She doesn't appreciate it and no matter how hard I try; she doesn't understand me."

Monica was quiet. I let a tear escape as I tried to turn away from her. She used her hand to turn my face to her so she can wipe away my tear. She gave me a heart-felt expression and spoke, "L. T. I am here for you if you need me. I understand all too well how it is to have the one you love leave you or be used by someone. I am a prime example of love can go band. Let us just take whatsoever we call this and go slow. You and your thing about your wife and me and my trust issues have to be dealt with straightforward before we can move forward. I need my next relationship to be more stable."

"I understand and I am completely with you on that. It's like they don't see how good they have it. It's like we give and give to see nothing in return." I spoke to get on her level.

"You know my husband wasn't always a dead beat. He used to do things for me and the children but he stop talking to me and started talking to other women. Before I knew it, we did more arguing than talking. It's like he would get angry at me and go be happy with them. But see, they don't live with him and they don't expect him to do much a nothing for them. Here in this house we have bills, kids and responsibilities. We can't ha-ha and he-he all the time. I guess that I just wasn't what he wanted anymore."

Placing my arms around her, I whispered, "In the end, we are the ones that win."

"Oh here. We got caught up in our affairs and I forgot to offer you the snack" She said with laughter.

"It's all I have here" Monica went on and said.

"You don't have food here?"

"I have a little."

Without saying anything else, I reached in my wallet and handed her a hundred-dollar bill. She looked at me and said, "No. I will provide for me and my children. I need the money, but I feel like a whore that just sold herself."

"I understand but don't think of it that way. You and I were two lonely individuals that were in need of some loving. I give this to you because of the kids. I don't like to see children I know of personally hungry or without, if I can help them."

Swallowing a little, Monica took the money. She gave me an affectionate hug. Once she released me the words I heard was, "Thank you so much. You have helped me in my time of need each time I needed someone. I can't explain how I this feels to me. Men mostly want sex and not want to help me at all but you. L. T. you are different and for that I won't forget it."

I got up and she stood with me. We began walking towards the front door. Before I opened it I spoke, "It's getting late and I have to get to my other business arrangement. Are you going to be alright, when I leave?"

"Sure I will be fine and I will sleep like a baby, thanks to you."

"No thanks to you, I feel good. I needed that sexing."

The woman reached up and I leaned into her kiss. It was brief. I broke the interaction and walked off thinking *now she knows I am here for her and now I can get that ass as often as I like.* I got in the car and checked my cell phone. Solo called. I spoke out loud, "What the hell she want?"

"Hello" was her voice.

"I saw you called. Is everything ok?"

She was silent and when she is silent, that means I am not going to like what comes out her mouth. My wife said, "I came by the house earlier to see you because I miss seeing your face. You weren't there."

"Yeah, I was on some business. I'm on my way back to the house now."

"Oh, ok but where were you?"

"Didn't I say I was on some business? You act like, I'm not grown. Shit, Solo I wasn't born with a twin; in fact, I don't even need my own shadow. What has gotten into you?"
"You have gotten into me. Since I've been away, I see things differently."

Boy what I tell you was OG Pete's voice in my head.

"Differently how?"

"I can't explain it but it's like I see another side of you."

"That doesn't explain why you came over. You haven't told me that."

"It doesn't matter. You weren't there for me so it'll be ok."

"Solo you playing damn mind games." I said as I arrived at the hotel where Lizzie was at.

"Babe we both know you are the biggest gamer of us all and you talk about me? Remember before I got to where I am at now, I played the game you played.
I didn't hear anything else she said because I heard that catch phrase from OG Pete, *Watch that dog that brings that bone; if he's bringing one, he's carrying one.*
"Did you even hear me?"

"Babe cut the bullshit. You want to leave say so. Don't come at me with shit you don't really know about."

"You saying I don't know about the streets?"

"No, you don't know about me."

"In spite of what you may think, I love you and I want you to leave the streets alone, have a family and go to church."

"Here we go again."

"That's right; here we go again about the same stuff. I have been screaming all these years about slowing down. Can't you see that the enemy wants to keep us separated by having you in the streets and less with me?"

"All I can see is no light bill being paid, no nice car, no business and no damn money! That's what the fuck I see, when I don't see the streets. If you knew any better you would see the same vision I see."

Solo was pissing me off. I haven't raised my voice with her in a long time and tonight she was getting it. My wife then spoke in a calm manner, "L. T. you have never raised your tone to me and when I talk about you being committed to me you get angry. Those people and your shop gets more attention and love than I do. Mudcat gets more love than I do."

"This is about other women, isn't it?"
"No, it's about you slowing down, going to church and starting a family."

"What does going to church have to do with me slowing down?"

"Your back door shop wouldn't exist and we can have God in our lives."

"Just because I have a back door operation doesn't mean I don't have God. This is about you thinking I am having affairs."

"I put everything aside to have a normal life not to have a husband that lived in the streets more than he lived at home. I can tell you are hearing me and not listening. You know what forget I ever called."

"No Solo you listen to me. You don't think pussy comes at your dick all day every day? Do you know how many women I have turned down? If I want to fuck guess what I am going to do? I am going to fuck! You can't stop me if that is what I want to do but it is not. You are my wife, and I will go to church in time."

Before Solo hung up she said, "Since you like old sayings how about this one, don't let the hearse bring you to church."

I know damn well she didn't just throw one of OG Pete's saying at me. Smiling, I looked at the phone and put it back on silent. *While she is gone, I have to get on my grind so I can get her back.* I thought as I got out the car and knocked on the suite door.

When the door swung opened, it was Lizzie. Smelling good as hell but I was not in the mood. Solo, and all her talk about church has gotten to me. Closing the door behind me I said, "Babe you smell good."

"I can tell you have something on your mind because of the way you greeted me."

"Yeah, I do but right now I need to hold someone that cares about me."

I pulled off my shoes and got in the bed. Lizzie got in front of me and I held her. I have to make the bitch think she is the one woman besides my wife that I talk to and right now she was eating it up.

"I am here for you L. T. if you want to talk about it."

"I do want to talk. I need to know if you know how my wife gets a recording of the three of us."

Lizzie turned towards me to say, "I would never jeopardize what we have. I know you have a wife, and I know you have me but if she found out anything you need to look farther than me. Why would I get you in trouble? If you get in trouble than means I will have to pay rent and get a man. The main reason for no trouble would mean no you and I don't want to lose you."

"The last part is a damn no-no. I am the only one you fucking. I can't have anybody else taking pleasure in the loving you give me." I said as I pulled her closer to my face.
"Is that right?"

"Hell yeah, that's right, you my woman."

"I know and it makes me feel good to hear that."

Lizzie leaned over to kiss me but her cell went off. She pulled back and picked it up from the desk. In a demanding tone, I spoke, "Who the fuck calling you while I am with you?"

She said, "Here, it's for you."

"For me?"

"Yeah, it's Mudcat."

I got the phone from her and said, "What's up man?"

"Shit I need you to come get me?"

"Where the hell are you?"

"Right now, I am in holding and they may lock me up but the Chief knows I work for you so he told me to tell you to come down and get me."

"I'm on my way."

The Chief and I go way back to my grandfather OG Pete days. He doesn't fuck with me or my operation because he knows that I have all types of shit on him and it could give him the same time other motherfuckers get. This works out for me because I can keep on doing what I do as long as I keep the legit business by paying taxes. I gave Lizzie back the phone and she said, "You leaving aren't you? He calls and leaves me."

"Yeah, my boy needs me."

"Hell, I need you."

Reaching for Lizzie I kissed her, and I touched her face. I love the way she pouts and it is a turn on but right now I have to go. *As if she doesn't know my three B's: Business-Before-Bitches.* I can get pussy any time as long as I have money or goods.

"When you coming back?"

"I may return tomorrow sometime. It's late and I'm not going to want to drive all the way here."

"You right baby. I know you are tired, and you need your rest."

"Right."

I got up and put my clothes back on. Shit I was tired as hell and having too much shit going on. Now my wife is tripping, I have to get this shit together so she can bring her ass back home. As of now, I need to see what the hell going on with my boy.

Once I arrived at the Shore County Jail, I walked in. I told the dispatcher who I was and I signed my name for Mudcat to be released. He came out looking like he has been on a field trip and not in holding cell. I asked him, "What the hell happened?" I questioned him as he grin his grin that says, yeah I fucked up.

"Man lets go. We can talk in the car."

"Where yo shit at?"

"That pig motherfucker impounded it. I'll get it out tomorrow."

We went to my car and he got in. I began to drive off before asking, "What the fuck you do?"

"I whipped that stanking bitch ass."

"Whoa back the fuck up. What you mean you put your hands on a woman?"

"I know you don't think a man needs to hit a woman, but shit let me tell you."

"I met this shorty, and we were kicking it. I was spending my cash on her and we decided to go back to her house. I was uneasy but the bitch was saving me some money. I was gone on that drank and ready for some ass. She smelled good and shit I couldn't wait to fuck her."

"What is the problem?"

"I pulled off my clothes and she pulled off hers. She started sucking on this dick while I was still drinking. You know how damn good that shit feels, minus the drinking because you don't drink."

"If she mobbing on that head just right, hell yeah that shit good as hell."

"Anyway, I decide to eat the pussy, fuck it. I get between her legs and threw the covers off me. I kept stopping and fanning and getting mad as hell."

"For what?"

"The damn flies tried to take the pussy from me."

"What the hell you say?"

"Yo ass heard me. The damn flies tried to take over the stanking ass pussy from me."

I kept on laughing and laughing as he said, "I ain't lying. At first, I thought it was me, so I even put alcohol in my mouth to numb the smell and that shit didn't stop those damn flies for wanting the pussy I tasted. I kept on taking her pussy in my mouth, but they began to fucking take me down. I got up swinging and her ass got hit a few times in the process."

As hard as I laughed, I cried out to say "Boy, don't you eat her ass again."

"Shit you don't have to worry about that. When I came to my senses, her ass was bleeding and shit. She was hollering and going on; I didn't know what the hell was wrong. I should have been the one hollering. Flies were chasing me because her stanking ass pussy was in my mouth."

"How the police get called?"

"She called them because she thought I had gone mad."

"What the police say?"

"They laughed and she got pissed off. They told me they would have my car removed from her premises and being that I had been drinking I had to come with them and have someone come get me."

We arrived back to my house. I glimpsed the time on my phone, and it was almost four am. We got out and I unlocked the door. The minute we were inside, I went straight to the fridge. I thought out loud, "Times like this make me miss my wife."

My boy added as he fixed a bowl of cereal, "There is nothing like coming home to a woman that loves you."

"All I had to do was come in and she would get up and fix me something to eat but most of the time I didn't bother her."

"L. T. you have it all."

"How the fuck is that?"

"Your house paid for and all your shit is yours. You don't owe no damn body."

"Yeah, but I don't have my wife."

"True but she will be back."

"I hope so."

"If she doesn't, you still can get pussy any time of the day. Pussy just comes to yo ass like its nothing."

"Pussy is a soft, wet piece that every woman has but every woman won't love you for you."

Slowly Mudcat said, "I know you miss her ass."

"Hell yeah I do. We been together through it all and she knows me like I know her, but she wants me to give up this way of living."

"Why don't you?"

"You try giving up everything you have ever known for the unknown. I don't want to be that struggling man that works all his life and doesn't have shit to show for it."

"That is some deep shit."

"Shit I been there and done that. It wasn't cool at all."

"Now, for a Nigga like me, it wouldn't be too hard, because I ain't ever had shit. This is the best I have lived in all my life and I have you to thank you. Shit if yo ass hadn't taken a chance on me I might be in prison by now for dealing dope, if not dead."

"Let me spit this to you. It pays to be like me, a jack of all trades. I can paint cars, houses, boats you name it I can paint it. Strip down cars, draw pictures on anything or anybody part, do air brushes, buy this, sell or trade that. I can survive on the streets because I am good with my hands."

"It pays to be up on the game and dope too if you got it."

"Dope connections ain't shit but jail time, Mudcat. I've partook my share of pushing in big kilos and I have stashed back much of that for rainy days."

"Rainy day my ass, you acting like yo ass on a legal job."

"Not all of it is legal but dope is serious. I saw how my family got fucked up in the process of dealing drugs. That was a way of living is good as hell but if I can make my business other ways I will. I'm good with graffiti and shit, not nickeling and diming or heavy weight."

"I like the operation you have here. It's steady and the money is damn good."

After I finished eating my warmed up pizza, I said, "But you know what, a dope boy can't hustle. If you take away the dope his ass is grass. He only knows how to deal dope or hit a lick here and there but a hustler; his ass can make money all types of ways. A hustler is what I am. If you take away one skill, I have others to fall back on."
"Shit if you take stripping down cars from me, I ain't go shit but a hard dick and sometimes it doesn't want to get hard."

I laughed and Mudcat said, "Why won't you drink sometime? I don't ever see you take a swallow."

"OG Pete always said you can't think with a cloudy mind and drinking messes with your judgment. When on that liquor you never know when or where you have to deal and how you going to deal if you aren't thinking clearly? Plus I never required the taste for alcohol or dope. In fact, I've never smoked dope and only taken a few drinks of liquor that I can remember."

"Man, you my fucking hero" Mudcat said as he ate more cereal.

"Good night, man. A Nigga tired, done fucked down and have to go to bed."

"Aight, don't wake me in the morning and I won't wake you." Mudcat said as I walked out the kitchen and to my lonely bedroom.

CHAPTER 7

When I finally opened my eyes it was very early Monday morning. I could not believe that I slept all day Sunday and hadn't heard from Mudcat. I was glad because I didn't feel like talking. I have a lot on my mind and have to do some thinking then my stomach growled.

I got up and fixed me something to eat and saw Mudcat's car was at the shop. I walked outside and opened the door to see if he was there. On my large, deep couch were some damn girl and Mudcat. My friend must have heard the door, "See I didn't wake yo ass up and you slept all day Nigga."

"Hell yeah, I've slept all day. I was tired."

"I guess. You must have been worn out."

"I was tired as hell and not worn out, there's a difference."

The girl woke up and got up wearing only her tan skin and straight black hair. I didn't mean to look because she was with my boy but fuck she saw me and got up. *Bitches like that will cry wolf on yo ass in a minute.* Trying to see where I knew her from, then it hit me. I remembered her from Dandy's job. I also remembered how I've fucked her a while back. The remembrance of that day placed a huge grin. She smiled as she asked, "You live here?"

"Yeah" I said as I eyed her slender body.
"I'm thirsty."

"I only have water."

"L. T. her ass doesn't want water. She wants to drink two Vitamin D milk shakes."

"Is that right?" I turned to her and asked.

"That's if you want me to give you a little something to wake you up."

"Hell yeah man. You know she gives good head" Mudcat spoke as he positioned himself for her to taste him.

"Naw man you go on, do you. I have dollars on my mind and I don't need distractions. You on the other hand needs to hurry up we have some orders to fill by eleven."

"The way she sucks I will be finished in five minutes."

As I began to walk into my office she got between his legs and began tasting him. When I looked to my right I saw a little camera. I forgot that my boy is a damn freak, and he gets off on watching himself in action.

I checked my phone again and saw Dandy had called. I checked her voice mail, and it said, "Why yo ass didn't pick up the phone and shit? Yo damn wife not there. What the hell you doing? Hit me back up, hell bye."

I decided not to call her back not just yet; going to make her wait. I opted to check inventory parts and to see what is on the menu and I have a '00 Mercedes and a '95 Chrysler coming in from the South. Hearing Mudcat grunt loudly, I peeped out the office window that leads to the shop to see if they were finished.

I didn't see them. This time, I opened up the door and walked into the shop area. They were letting the shop air out as they stood in the door. Mudat yelled out, "Boss! I'll be back?"

Standing by the right, was Mudcat and the girl. I walked out and spoke, "Ok, you know you have work to do."

"I got to get my new shorty home."

"Go on" I said as I turned back and went into my office.

About half an hour later Mudcat came back and he started taking a motor out of a car. I started priming a Volkswagen that has to be painted in the next day for a man's high school daughter's present. When I came out the process room my dealer was waiting with the two cars from the South rolled in. We did our exchanges and he left.

Mudcat and I decided to take a break and go to Subway. We ordered our food and left. While I was out, I went by the Lawyer's office that Monica told me about to give her the money and sign the papers for her house to be mine. While I was there, I signed it back over to her for her and her children and felt good in the process.

Motherfuckers like her husband needs to be ashamed because those are his children. It's bad enough but there are stupid bastards out there, that can't count any damn way. They will leave their woman and their one or two kids for a woman with three or more. What the hell! You decrease your situation not increase it. If her ass has more children than you and you didn't do shit for the one's you fathered, what makes a woman and some men think the new children will be taken care of? Like I said, we men do some fuck up shit and the shit her kids dad is doing is one of them.

I came out the office and we went back to the shop kitchen and began to eat. My friend said, "You know, I really like your set up and how you got things going?"

"What is there to like? You can have your own thing like me."

"Yeah but the way you operate and all your connections are legit. I can't get that."

"I hustled hard coming up and I didn't spend my money foolishly. You have to set yourself goals and a time frame to accomplish them."

"That shit doesn't work."

"I am proof that it does work. You have to put your mind to it and follow through with it even if it gets hard and you want to splurge, don't."

"I have expensive habits, but I have been talking to this one woman and she may be worth it."

"Well until you kick your women, alcohol and high roller lifestyle you won't be able to get on your feet. But is this is a good woman and she isn't playing with your head go for it. Maybe she will make you hold onto your money."

"She will but the problem is has a man and they been together for a while, but I want to be her man."

When I heard him say she has a man I decided to spit a little game because I know my boy is another Putty Tang loving pussy and women. I decided to enlighten him by saying, "You know I fuck them and don't love them. I don't give a damn about those women but where is my next dollar coming from. To hear she has a man is a problem. For starters, her ass can't be faithful and that is one of the qualities you look for in a real woman, if you are to be serious about her. If she cheating on him she's cheating on you and if she is using him, I bet this shop she is using you."

"True. I understand what you are telling me."

From the way he said that, I knew he did not believe me. I then said, "I am happy for you. I don't want you to be taken for a fool because women will play with your heart and use your head as a sex toy to fuck with. They are just as ruthless and cut throat as I am. To be honest, my grandfather sat me down and explained to me about women and not only did he sit me down he drilled me for days at a time about women. A lot of my intake on women comes from years of experience and studying a woman. I can walk in a room and tell if a woman is taken she is or if she is on the prowl. It's all in their body language. It takes years of knowing and observing and experience plays a key factor in it."

"I believe ya and I don't care if she has a man the pussy too good, unless I dreamed it was good."

"If you are dreaming if it's good, then she is not really fucking you. She is playing some type of game to let you think she is fucking you. She is either telling you, you fucked her after you wake up or it's really good and it makes you dream you were fucking her. Either way, I don't think you are getting the pussy like you think. As for her other man, what is she going about him?"

"I don't know but she said she is going to let him know that she has moved on."

"Don't let a woman do to you, what I do to them?"

With his eyes wide, he said, "Nigga you do some ruthless ass shit to them bitches."

"I don't do to them, what they don't want done. It's all a part of the game we play every day. Everything begins with a thought. It starts in the brain then when it forms outside the brain, that thought now has life. That forming could be emotionally or physically, either way they form. When they form it takes a matter of time before bullshit forms out your mouth. Understand the concept, that flirting can lead to fucking. Conversations and being a friend leads to falling for the guy and then fucking. Once a woman gets to thinking about you she begun to fall for you without consciously admitting it, then you fucking. It is when she is alone or when you send her nice words and even calls her to check on her sooner or later, you fucking. Shit like that is what they love and if they love it, you fucking.

You see fucking is what comes from many friendships, especially if that is what's on your mind. You can't be a statistic in the game that was created by a woman."

"How is that?"

"Didn't Eve make Adam eat that apple?"

He didn't say anything. I went on and asked, "Have you not read the first story in the Bible?"

I waited on him to say something, and he didn't. Trying to make a long story short, I went on to say, "Anyway for her to make that man eat that apple she had to have some game or power of persuasion. He supposed to be the leader, but she took the position and made her mind up to eat. She tasted it and lured Adam into eating it."

"You always give me some type of story."

"All I am saying is women started the game so we men have to be on top of the game. Get them before they get you."

"L. T. that is all you have to say. Yo ass started talking about a woman I only heard about in church."

"I just don't want you to be persuaded and mislead by pussy. I don't want you to think with your smaller head, that's all but what are you going to do?"

"Get my weight up so I can have just as much money as the next man. When I do this she gonna have to let him go or let me go."

"Having a good woman by your side will encourage you. Shit Solo has been there for me and there isn't anything I wouldn't do for her. At the same time, I watch my heart. I can live without her, right now I chose not to. You see, pussy is like dick, you can get it a dime a dozen but when it comes to making a woman your wife, and the shit gets real fuck the dozen."

"Well Solo wants you to give up the illegal part of your business."

"Like I told her, I am trying to make a certain amount of money, and I don't plan to quit until that quota is met. Then I will leave it alone because I think it would be a substantial amount to support a family way of living. It is true I could quit now and be ok. But I want to be more than ok. I want to be well off. If I want to take my wife on an expensive trip to the UK or pay in full college tuitions or things like that, I can do that without putting this and that back. I saw how partying and not being smart could ruin a person, like it did to everyone in my family but OG Pete."

We didn't talk too much until I heard him say, "You know Solo is a remarkable woman and she just needs time to think."

"Yes, she is. I plan to give her all that time but if she is going to be with me she will, if not she won't. My grandfather always told me don't ever let a woman know that you can't live without her and Solo is a woman that I can't live without but I will; if the need be. Besides I saw this house she wanted, and I got it for her but not sure when to tell her."

"That's good but are you sure that with you is where she belongs?"

I heard him talk about Solo and it isn't until now that I hear something in his words. In that instant, OG Pete words rang loudly, *where there's smoke, there's fire.* Pushing them back I spoke, "It may not be where she belongs, but I hope this is where she belongs. If she wants to play games and give the pussy away fuck it. She can give it to you or the next man it's her ass her pussy. I can't control it. If she wants to fuck, she will fuck no questions asked but she better not let me find out."

"Man I hope she comes on because I know you love her, and she loves you. I don't see her fucking anyone else but you."

We continued to eat. Once we finished, we tidy up the kitchen and went back to work. I checked my cell phone and went in the office. Deeply I yearned to call Solo but know she values space. I took a seat in my chair and thought, *when a woman asks for space she is sending out a silent cry for help. It is almost like a woman being silent when she is engrossed in thought. However, during this time men must give her that space but continue to do things for her to remain on her mind. You don't ever want her to be away from you and not think about you. It is at this separation that you keep her focused on you so no other man has time to step in while she is in her thinking process.*"

I called to the florist in her sister's hometown. Using my Visa card I ordered her a dozen of Daisy's her favorite flower. She is going to be surprised. Then it hit me, tonight I go see Dandy at the club. Soon as that idea came out, my office phone rung. Another order of vehicles was coming in and I had to be here to get it. My connections are really on it by getting at me and getting my paper up.

Opening up the office door, I waved for Mudcat to come over and he did. Before he got close, he asked, "What's up?"

"If you have plans cancel them because we have to stay a little later tonight."

Mudcat gave me a serious face as he asked, "We must have some ASAP work?"

"We do and it has to be out by the morning."

"That's what I am talking about. You always on the paper chase."

"You have to if you have a goal and a time frame like I said earlier."

"Ok. Let me finish this job up."

He and I went our separate ways. He back to the shop area and I back to the office to do the legal side of the paperwork. About another hour passed and I finished up my office work and Mudcat finished up his body work. All we had to do now was wait on the next shipment to come in so we can work.

"What you have planned for tonight?" Mudcat asked as he came into my office.

"I have plans to go see Dandy at the club, but money comes first."

"Can you help me get on?"

"If you feel you can handle the legal side of the paperwork."

"Hell no. I'm talking about the stripping downside."

I looked at him. He seems anxious to be on his own so I tried him by saying, "Mudcat you can't have an open chop shop. You have to have a legal business which requires paperwork to be done, then your chop shop in the back like mine."

"The woman I was telling you about works uptown at the Court House. She knows about that kind of shit."

"You trust this woman?"

"Yeah, I do."

"Does she know of these plans of yours and does she know that it is the illegal side of the law?"
"She does."

"I trust your opinion and if that is what you want. Make sure your business is away from mine."

"Man, mine going to be in another town."

"When you plan to do this?"

"Don't really know but I hope soon."

"Well let me know and I will see what I can do."

Mudcat grinned like a damn woman that just heard sweet bullshit. I will help him, but I will make sure my name is not tied to his, in case his ass gets caught by not doing the shit right. Hell, I can't afford for any of my long time clients to get caught but if they want to try it that is up to them. My cell phone rang and it was Dandy. Mudcat left out the office and went inside the shop area.

"Hello."

"Why didn't yo ass call me back, yo ass know I called you. Shit is yo ass still coming or what?"

"It amazes me how ghetto YO ASS talks. It keeps me laughing and the pussy is on point. I may be late coming by it all depends on when I finish here at the shop."

"Why didn't yo ass call me back?"

"I don't have to answer to you."

"True, true yo ass doesn't answer to me and when you want pussy, she won't answer to you."

"I am going to tell you what I want and you better tell your pussy to give it, when I want."

She was silenced and so was I. Dandy broke the barrier to say, "I don't get off til two. Bring your ass because I will need a ride home."

"If I am finished I will come. When I get there, you better not have another fucker in your face and lap dancing is out."

"Yo ass doesn't pay all my bills. Shit I give you money, hell. I have to do what I have to do."

"No lap dancing when I am there and that is all I have to say."

Soon as I said that, Mudcat was at the door; which, meant I have a visitor. Walking in behind him was Solo. I began to smile for I missed her. Letting Dandy know that her time was up, I said "I will see you later, my wife is here."

"Damn she back home?"

"Bye."

Mudcat left us alone. I stood up and went around to her. I skimmed my wife's face, and it looked just as gorgeous as the first day I met her. Her face was as radiant as her eyes. I almost forgot how beautiful she was until this moment. Her yellow dress was simple, but she makes it look expensive; just by being in it. The way the ruffles displayed around her slender shoulders and warm skin, the invitation to touch her was too inviting. The impulse to be with her became overwhelming as I continued to adore the woman I married.

Sometimes being a man doesn't mean you have to be a dog, it just means you have to be a respectable dog. No matter how much I love her, I love the streets too so I fuck them and everything in it. Solo used the tip of her fingers to paint on the inside of my palm, to break my inner thoughts of how much I love her. She knows that I am recalling in my mind about her and how she appears to me this today.

Women like the build-up the momentum of sex. They want you to the point where you can't think of anything else but them and what they plan to do to you that night. From the sexual scent of their perfume to their, luring way they dress you can't help but be anxious for them. At this point, you are ready and the only thing you think of is getting them in the bed.

Focusing on Solo, I saw Mudcat smile as he left out the door. With her fingertips still in my palm, I knew this was our signal for sex. Immediately I am still aroused and waiting to see what the next move will be.

"I came by to see you, to touch you because I've missed you so."

Coming closer so nothing is between us but air, I spoke truthful, "And I've missed you deeply. Did you like the flowers?"

"I'm here aren't I?"

Taking her fingertips she began to make trails all up my arm and onto my shoulders as she walked around me. This move of hers has left a tingling sensation throughout my entire body. She knows that I don't like the tease but having it done by her, it's worth it. The temptress wife of mine, sat down with her short skirt that exposed her toned honey coffee thighs. Turning to her, I wrapped my arms around her and that felt better than anything I could have imagined.

Pleasing as it is to smell her I tighten my grip and placed paths of light kisses all over her neck. Those tender kisses were memorable and genuine even the light strains her hair that usually gets in my way turned me on. Solo reached up and placed her hands onto my arms and swayed leisurely. I smiled because I know that this tactic is to get me into thinking what it would feel like to have her beneath me. It was working.

I began to imagine her naked and hungry for what I have to offer. Plain as day I began to remember our sex life and how so much I need her and not Dandy or the others. This attraction between us was more played out and more seductive than any before. I have to give it to my wife, the bitch is good.

"Are you still thinking about me and sex?"

"I am always thinking about you and sex."
"Well hold me for a little bit longer, if you don't mind."

Letting her go was the last thing I was doing. I could not pry my arms off her, even if I wanted too. Her skin is soft and the aroma she was giving me was sex. I got to get her back home.

"Go on L.T. and sit down in your desk."

"What if I don't want to sit down?"

"You don't have too but I do want to see more than your arms around me."

Getting up, I took my seat across from her. She smiled her famous smile at me, and I was hooked. You talking about being led by the nose, this woman had me by the mouth, eyes, ears and throat too.

"Quit drooling, I'm still your wife."
"Yeah, and do you know how long it has been since I've been this close to you? You make a man do crazy things."

"Well, I came by to see you and to see have you given much thought about living a normal life with me?"

I was silent because I miss having her in my arms and my bed, I just can't let go of this way of living. Giving her an honest reply, I said "I have been thinking about it but I haven't done it."

She got up and I ran over to her to say, "Babe it's not like I don't want to. I have been trying to get a little more money so I can quit."

"L. T. it matters not to me about a little more money because that little more money will only have you needing a little more money and the cycle will continue."

"You are right, but I aspire to give you top of the line everything."

"Get it through your thick skull. I don't need the top of the line anything. I only need you and only what you can give but what you are telling me is that, I am not important enough in your life for you to let it go."

When she said let it go, I remembered Lizzie and how she was acting when I was on top of her. It's funny to be with one woman and thinking about the other woman but it is Lizzie's words that brought back a memory how she can give me the freedom my wife won't.

"I love the shit out of you. Solo, you are important, but this is for our future."

"Wrong. It's for your future. Don't contact me until you are ready for a real wife and family."

She walked off and the way her hips moved, I couldn't help but stare; even though, she just gave me an ultimatum. Evidently, she doesn't know who she is married too. Before opening the door, she halted in her tracks just like Dandy did to say, "Don't make me wait too long for if you do, I could be gone."

Solo closed the door and like that she was gone. I went back to my seat and began replaying the conversation. I entwined my fingers and placed them in front of me. This was my pose for almost an hour. I heard a car pull up. Removing my hands, I got up and checked the window on the side. Solo is just now leaving. Moments later, Mudcat went back to work. I walked to his area and asked, "What were you two talking about?"

"She wants me to talk some sense in you."

I stared him up and down as he started back working. He is my boy but pussy is powerful, and women know they have that kind of power just don't know how to use it. However, Solo does. Asking again, I spoke "What did you tell her?"

"I told her that you love her and you doing what you think best for you and her. She was like but I don't care for the finer things I only care for him. I told her to give you a little more time to get what you trying to do and if that doesn't work then ya do what ya need to do."

"Ok. The merchandise will be here in a few. I want to work fast. I have to go see Dandy."

"Let a Nigga go with ya."

"Why would I go to a strip club without my favorite boy?"

"Yo ass better not. You know all the pussy that works there."

"I haven't fucked all them either, maybe one or two."

My office phone rung and I wasn't going to answer it but decided to anyway. It was Monica. I pronounced, "Hello."

"Hi, it's me Monica."

"How you doing?"

"Great. I was not sure if I should call but I took the chance anyway."

The phone was silent and as I waited for her to get the real reason why she was calling me, off her chest. Soon as that thought came, she spoke with a weary tone, "I just want to thank you for saving our home. You don't know how much I appreciate it."

"You're welcome."

"L.T. I am serious. We finally have a place to stay and it is because of your idea. The children and I want to cook dinner for you, if that's ok?"

"Sure that sounds good, when?"

"How about tomorrow evening if you don't have any plans?"

"That's sounds great. Is there anything in particular I need to wear, jeans, what?"

"Anything you wear will be fine, just dress comfortable."

"Well jeans it is. I look forward to seeing you and the children. How are they anyway?"

"They good and they been asking about you?"

"That's wonderful to hear."

"Yeah, it is but on a personal level, I can't wait to see you. I mean you've stirred something up in me and it's not dying down."

"I hope not because you are doing something to me and to know that the children like me and I like them all is truly great. I don't have children and to play with yours and teach them how to do things is an honor to me, for that I thank you Monica."

"It means more to me than you know to have a man like you in our lives. You are what we need."

"It's good to know you feel that way and wear something sexy. I want to spend time with the children and keep my eyes on you."

She giggled like a schoolgirl with a crush as she spoke, "I sure will. Bye."

CHAPTER 8

I hung up the phone as Mudcat and I went in the house. It was late. I have to make an appearance to make Dandy think she is that important to me. Mudcat and I arrived at Dandy's job. The place was half packed. Women were on the stage dancing and looking good as hell but my objective for the night is to make Dandy think I am into her. We walked around and got a table upfront. Mudcat ordered beer and wings. I only ordered a dry coke with ice.

Someone must have told Dandy that I was here because she came out the back strutting like a prize. I must say, she is beautiful in her own way but to see her out here I smiled because I knew me being here was working. Check this out.

If a man has a ghetto bitch, he has to show interest. He has to make her think that she is everything that the wife is not and naturally it is true. This type of woman must feel like you have feeling for her and that you are protective of her; as if she was a wife. You must have her to believe that she is wife material for you; even though, you know she is not. Although, all women want to be special and almost all should be treated as such.

Before Dandy could make it my way, my cell went off and it was Lizzie. I was kind of thrown off because she hardly ever calls me, I call her. I lifted my finger to Dandy for her to wait a minute but the look she gave me was trouble. Walking outside, I answered the call.

"Hello."
"Hi."

"Yeah, you called?"

"Yeah, I just wanted to know what's up because you haven't been with me in a while."

"That's what you contacted me for?"

"Yeah, I need you L. T."

"People in hell need ice water but they ain't getting it."

"It's just that it has been a minute since I saw you, is all I'm saying."

"Are your bills getting paid?"

"Yes."

"Are you lacking for anything?"
"Other than you, no."

"Well shut the fuck up. You the only woman I have other than my wife. So, shit be patient and let pencil you in. You know I have to get that money to continue the lifestyle you adore so much."

"Yeah, you right. I'm just lonely and you are my only man."

She is right. I do need to spend some time with her, but I have been so busy with Solo and trying to make this money. Taking a breath, I spoke, "You right. I'm sorry babe. I've been busy trying to make this bread. I do have to take care of you and shit."

"Ok just make some time for me that all I'm saying."

"You right babe. No matter how busy I am, I do need to make time for you, and I promise that I will do just that."

"Ok, can't wait to see you."

"You too. Let me go back in here and finish what I was doing."

"Good bye."

"I will see you later."

I turned my phone on vibrate and went back in. When I got back inside, Dandy was giving some Nigga a lap dance. I just stood there and watched the show. I was far from furious because I am not stupid. I know that she is no more to me than the rest of the hoes I mess off with. Smiling I decided to show my ass for her. Mudcat saw my expression, and he knows what I am thinking. I came over to Dandy and stood there as she was dancing with her back to the guy. She saw me and continued to dance more seductive than ever.

Being a woman like she is, I knew she was angry because I walked out before she came over to me. In her mind, I took another woman's call over seeing her first; which, I did. However, that is why she is doing what she does, to try and make me jealous. It was not working at all but I have a role to play just like everybody else in the streets.

"What the hell is this?" I snapped to Dandy with Mudcat on my side.

She continued to dance. *Now this ghetto ass bitch is about to make me go to level two,* I thought as I snatched her off the guy's lap.

"Wait one damn minute. I've paid for her time" the guy screamed out.

"L. T. I know damn well you not trying to start some shit on my damn job!"

"L. T.!" The guy spoke.

"Yeah?"

"Man, I'm sorry" He said as he walked off.

"What the hell is yo ass trying to prove?"

"I said no lap dancing, and I mean no lap dancing."

"How the hell am I to make those dividends if you here cutting the fuck up?"

"Because you are my woman and I can take care of yo ass if I need too."

"If you keep this shit up, yo ass gonna have to put up or shut the fuck up."

"Fucking lap dance again like that, if you bad; for when you do, I will show more than my ass."

Dandy didn't like it one bit as she yelled out to me, "I am not your wife, I'm your bitch and I can quit you any fucking time I choose!"

"You don't quit and I don't fire! Now like I said, fucking lap dance to another motherfucker again, in my face."

I walked off as she began acting angry. Taking another seat, I began to watch her. Everywhere she went the men would not let her lap dance while I was there. They know me and they know the kind of connections I pull. I am not violent, but I can only assume they think I represent The Times old way of doing things. Either way, it makes me no never mind.

Dandy was coming over to me. She had a smug look and Mudcat moved out the way. Dandy sat on my lap facing me. I love this position because in this angle she is at her best. She then said, "I need to make money tonight and since you are stopping my flow, pay me."

"You just give Mudcat a lap dance and I will see."

"I don't want to give his ass a fucking lap dance. That motherfucker doesn't have any money, shit he just be wasting my fucking time."

"I don't remember asking you too" I spoke soft enough for her to hear.

She got up and walked over to Mudcat. He was really stunned as he said, "What's this? A bottom bitch giving little ole, little bit dick me a lap dance?"
"It's not because I want to, so let's keep the shit straight."

I know her to be a tease, and I am going to see. She began to put her ass to in his face as her luscious breast faced me. The more she rolled her ass the more she showed off those breasts to me. In my opinion, she was working it and I was enjoying it. I know Mudcat loves it because she hasn't let him that close to her since the last time we fucked her.

Dandy then turned around and began bouncing her ass on my boy. I know he is hard because he lets pussy get him in trouble. I just love the way her ass moves up and down. It has been a minute since I've seen it from this view, and I miss it. However, she got up and my boy didn't want her to stop. He was getting too carried away.

"Lil Nigga get yo damn hands off me! It's time for my ass to get off."

"Come on, I have money to spend on yo ass tonight."

"But yo ass ain't what I want tonight."
He looked over at me and I said, "Come here Dandy."

She came over and I got up.

"Wait a minute Mudcat."

Dandy and I walked to the back. I led her to the room and said, "My boy wants to spend some money on that ass, let him."

"Shit all these other bitches here, get them."

"I will but right now he wants you."

"What am I going to get if I do so?"

"Bend over and let me get that nut out."

She smiled and said, "All I'm getting is a wet ass, is that right?"

"From me yes but from him a wet ass and some money, but right now I need to feel that pussy."

Like a bitch supposed to that listens to her man, she bent over and placed her hands on the low lying bar. I quickly dropped my pants. I entered her bare and it was good. I placed my fingers on each side of her inner thighs and began burying that dick in her. The more I pulled her ass to me the more I banged her pussy. It had been a minute since I hit her from the back and I liked it.

After a few more grinding sessions, I pulled out and nut splashed onto the carpet floor. I hadn't nut that quick in a while because I was on a time schedule. She went in the small washroom and used a towel to wipe off. Dandy then handed me a different towel. I wiped off and wiped my sperm from the floor.

She went in the washroom again, and gave me another towel so I could wrap the nut towel in. I don't leave my boys anywhere if I can help it.

"Damn L. T. yo ass was fast and I liked that shit."

"When we take you home tonight you fucking Mudcat."

"That little dick bastard? Why the hell you want to torture me like that?"

"He likes you and if you want this dick again you need to fuck yo ass off for him."

We walked out the room as if nothing happened. Dandy went towards the stage door, and I sat back in my seat. Mudcat got another dancer all over him and he was in his mode all I could do was stare at how he easily departs with his money. I must have been staring a long time because entering my thoughts was a voice saying, "Nigga snap the fuck out of it. We supposed to be enjoying bitches and shit but yo ass daydreaming and shit. Can't be about pussy because the place is crawling with that so what the fuck gives?"

"I thought about OG Pete."

"What the hell you thinking about him for?"
"Nothing at all, he just crossed my mind that's all."

"I'm drunk as hell and shit yo ass has to drive home. Hell, I can't even fuck but I can eat the pussy. Wait I will be sloppy doing that too" Mudcat spoke as he laughed.

"Dandy said you can stay the night at her house, unless you changing your mind?"

Laughing Mudcat slurred his speech to say, "Shit, I can't do a damn thing with that pussy but look at that big bitch. You know her pussy is a big bitch?"

"Yeah, but you better try something because she is yours for the night."

A different music came on and Dandy appeared on stage for it was her time to perform. I always love her on stage because it is there, she is alive and on her game. She flirts and makes the men throw cash to her but that does not bother her until I don't show up.

I didn't feel the need to cut the fuck up because I have her attention and knows my presence is strong. Dandy recognizes that when she is onstage, she only sees me, and my eyes are only on her. Tonight, my eyes didn't care for her, but I do know how to put on a front.

Back at our table, I continued to see Mudcat having fun with the dancer as one came towards us. It was the girl that was at my shop. She wore a red teddy that cuddled her in all the right places and those perky breast where bursting out at the seams as she elegantly came towards me. I must agree, she was stealing the show from Dandy, and I saw that Dandy didn't like that. However, she walked up to me and whispered softly, "May I dance for you?"

Before I can say anything, Mudcat stated, "Damn girl you look like a hoe dipped in cherry Kool-Aid. Let me drink yo ass up, I'm thirsty!"

She paid no attention to my boy, and he continued to let the entertainer entertain him. The seductress licked her lips, and I swore I saw fire because that is how hot she was. Politely I spoke, "That is ok. I have the dancer coming off the stage."

The dancer looked back at Dandy and said, "If you prefer ghetto bitches then she is it but me, I can be worth the while. I'm not trying to make you my man, I have one of those and neither am I trying to be your main girl because you have one of those but I tell you this; need I only to borrow you for a night? Maybe not tonight but just one night, you just tell me when. You know how to find me, ok?"

I smiled as Dandy was coming off the stage towards my table in the back. The dancer blew me a kiss as she turned to walk off. Dandy stopped her in her tracks. They spoke a few words and departed ways.

"Damn I thought those bitches were about to fight. I was about to see ass and breast swaying."

Having an accomplished feeling, I stated "Dandy is no damn fool. She knows I don't do that fighting shit."
The more I sat there the more I was relaxed. Mainly because of that nut from the room but all the same I was feeling damn good. Mudcat was acting like a kid in a candy store and that is one reason why he can be led by a piece of ass. He will give women everything he has and then some. In the end they

end up fucking him, with no Vaseline. I know he saw the way the girl looked at me as he asked, "Why yo ass always got to steal the women?"

I was taken aback by those words. In fact, stunned that he would wait until he got drunk to say that to me; however, being calm I spoke, "I don't take the women they come to me."

"Well, you need to stay in my married lane, and leave the other lanes to me."

I again was taken back his words again. This time I gander closer to my boy. He is drunk and is telling me that I have all the women. He is jealous, and from the use of his words this has been this on his mind for a while. Nicely again I asked, "My married lane?"

"Yes, when we out the hoes want you and they all seem to flock to you, and you think yo ass is the shit. You fuck this bitch and that bitch and then go fuck your wife. What the hell? Yo ass has a great thing at home and you fucking it up on bitches that don't mean shit."

This time I cleared my throat as I spoke, "My shit doesn't stink but it's my lane you are trying to get in."

"Just because yo ass has an education, money, can paint and bitches here and there don't make you the number one man. Somebody needs to knock you off your high horse."

Giving him my "what the fuck look" I coolly repeated his phrase, "I'm on a high horse, huh?"

Drinking some more he responded, "Hell yeah, you think yo ass can't be touched because you L. T. and you come from the infamous Times Family that has a legacy in crime and shit. But yo ass is coming down and yo wife leaving is the beginning."

Playing it cool, my response was, "It's the beginning, huh?"

"Hell yeah, you see your wife is the key to your success and I know she is the one bitch you protect above all others."

To keep him talking I said, "Yeah, she is. Keep going."

"You don't think her ass could be playing yo ass like the many women you play around this bitch? You don't think yo ass can get got, that's the problem right there nigga?"

"I can. I am not beyond my own game."

"Hell, yeah yo ass can but I have to give it to you. Yo ass got good ass game and bitches fall for it left and right. Shit I do a lot of yo shop work and I used to be down with yo ass like a dump truck with all four tires down but now you breaking hearts left and right. I want to break some hearts. You feel me?"
"Yeah, I do."

"Hell, yeah yo ass should."

"Do you wish you can be me?"

"To a degree but shit yo ass need to be brought down a motherfucking level."

Then as he said, "You way up here" he lifted his arm and hand above his head.

"But yo ass can be down here" When he said that he placed his arm and hand down by his feet, he waved them back and forth.

"You right" I spoke as I shook my head.

"Damn right, I'm right. Shit I have eyes I can see."

I didn't say anything more but I listen to him ramble on and on about shit in his heart. He doesn't know that when you are not influenced by alcohol you think clear and you remember clear. I've already told him that but he seems not to have listened. I've told him that you have to be on top of your game and you never know how things will fall. In fact, it was today that I told him all these things. He only sees me with all this, he has never seen the times when I hustled this and that just to make it. Sure I got a scholarship for Art but shit I still worked my ass off and maintain on the side. The shit was not easy.

However, the more I sat and listen to him talk, the more he has opened a new outlook to me. Mudcat is going to learn that you don't talk to me like that and you don't wait to get drunk. Out of nowhere I heard OG Pete's words, *"A drunken mind speaks what a sober mind feels."*

I grinned because it is so true. My boy, my best associate whom I took in is now showing me his real side. The best thing about it is, in the morning he won't remember he said that shit to me. This just reminds me of a game of chess, you wait for the right moment to make your move and Mudcat problem is he doesn't know how to move.

"Come on man, you're drunk. Let's go so you can get some rest."

"Man yo ass right. I am drunk as hell, but I do want to tap her ass. Here keep my money so her ass won't steal it."

This bastard reached into his wallet and gave me over two thousand dollars. I got it and said, "Cheers."

He lifted up his glass and he drunk some more; while, I drank dry coke. The more I said cheers the more he drank. I just sat back and watched this damn fool get wasted and how he just used the life rope to hang himself. Not soon enough, Dandy came out and was ready. We helped Mudcat to the car and we put him in the back seat. Before we got in I gave her a hug and spoke, "Change of plans."
"What?"
"You don't have to fuck him."
"I don't?"
"No. He's already fucked. Up." I slowly spoke to separate the words fucked up.

"Great."

"You can just tell him you did and that you couldn't handle it, that way he won't bug you often again about fucking."

"Hell yeah, I can't stand broke little dick Niggas."

"I know you are tired of him begging you for ass so I decided to help you."

"Yo ass has feelings after all."

We broke up the hugging and got into the car. I began to drive as he rode in half silence. The noise was coming from Mudcat's snoring and mumbling in his sleep. Before we got to Dandy's house, my rental property something said, "Look in your mirror at him."

I did then I heard, OG Pete say, *"Snakes come in all shapes, forms and colors. Look closely at him. He's a chameleon in a snake body."*

At that precise moment, Mudcat wiggled like he was trying to get comfortable but from this point of view he was moving like a snake. It was like a light blinded me and it made me see what I had never seen before. What I thought was no longer my thoughts.

We men know the kind of men we hang with and Mudcat is no exception. Men hate on each other just like women but to have my boy feel like this towards me, it's indescribable. The best thing about his outward confession is; I know how to play his cowardly ass; although, this night he has left an imprint on my mind, I will leave one on his heart.

The door opened, and I helped her get him in the house. We pulled off his clothes and put him in the bed. Dandy looked at me and spoke earnestly, "Are you going to stay? Yo ass got a small nut tonight you can have a bigger nut. I know I have gotten more out of you."

"You have but I have shit to do and I can't stay but we will talk again."

I closed the door and left her house. Deciding to go see Lizzie, I was going to surprise visit her and at three in the morning she better be alone.

Women don't understand that men don't like to be alone. We will move in the neighborhood slut or the town whore just to have a warm body to be beside us. We men don't need time to get over your ass, we move on to the next woman. It's just how it is. We don't mean to be unfeeling but it's something about not having a woman in our lives that scares the hell out of us.

That is how easy it is for a man to move in onto another relationship. We heal by having someone else there to replace you. With her there, we won't think about you as much and we won't miss you as much because we have a replacement for you. It doesn't mean we don't still want you, it just means we won't be alone.

CHAPTER 9

Turning off my thoughts, I turned into Lizzie's driveway, and her porch light was off; which, meant she was at home. I eased my car into park and sat there. My mind thought only about Mudcat and his confessions of his feelings toward me. I can now recall Solo's word about the only true friend is Jesus and everything else is an associate. Out loud I spoke, "You right baby, no true friends on this earth."

The thought of her almost made me sadden but I quickly reminded myself that she wanted to be away from me. While she is finding herself, I plan to find myself and maybe just maybe I will be finish with all these lies.

I got out the car and locked the doors. Once I made it to her front door, I used the key she gave me and not my rental key to open the door. Lizzie came from down the hall, turned on the light and said, "I had a feeling that you were coming."

"You did, huh?"

"Yeah, I did. Come here you. I've missed you."

Pulling Lizzie into my embrace was heartfelt. The smell of her skin was alluring as I held her tightly. She asked, "What's gotten into you?"

Leaning away from her so she could see my face, I spoke, "You and our relationship have gotten into me. I need to tell you I am sorry for standing you up the last time. It's just that it's been crazy around my way and shit money been coming left and right. You know I can't turn that down."

"You right. I'm just glad that you are here."

"I'm tired. I need to lie close to you and have you near me."

"We can do that."

She led me down the hall to her bedroom, I was gland of that. Her house is always clean, and she always smells good. When we got to her room, I pulled my shoes off and placed them along with my clothes in their place. I turned around and Lizzie was pulling her skimpy night coat off and revealing how full her body is. I smiled because she is beautiful and always pleasant to see.

Lizzie got on her side and me on mine. Once our bodies touched, I positioned my arms around her. She began to weep in small sounds, but I heard her and asked, "Babe what's wrong?"

She faced me and spoke, "I had an abortion."

I jerked up and turned on the light. I could not sit on the bed I continued to stare at her. Making sure, I heard her correctly, I asked, "What the hell you just say?"

Sitting up straighter in the bed, she stated again, "I had an abortion."

"What the hell you do that shit for? I mean are you fucking serious?"

"Yes. I was pregnant the last time we were together. I mentioned it and you told me to get rid of the motherfucker."

"Damn Lizzie, I wasn't fucking serious. I thought yo ass was making assumptions and I was just talking."

"You mean you weren't serious about aborting it?"

"Hell no! I don't believe in abortions that is why I try to make sure that getting a woman pregnant does not occur. I can't believe this shit. Why the hell didn't you contact me and talk to me? Why the fuck didn't you let me know what was up?"

Lizzie began to cry harder. I placed my arms around her because I know this must be devastating to her. She always wanted kids and now she has aborted a child she more than likely wanted. Parts of me was happy because that would be one less thing to explain to Solo, but the other half wanted to punch her in her damn face for not letting me in on a decision as that one.

"It's ok Lizzie. I wished you got in touch with me so you wouldn't have gone through this alone. I am here for you. Don't ever think I am not here for you."

She stopped crying then said, "I didn't know what to do. I wanted to keep it but I knew that you were still hoping your wife came back. If she did then our child would have complicated your life as well as mine; by that I felt it would have been selfish on my part. You see if I had the child I would have wanted you here with us all the time and not with your wife. I know us doing what we are doing is just that, doing something. I know it could not be serious but fuck. L. T. I fell for you and have always loved you."

I made up my mind to be her friend by stating, "You mean the world to me, and what we have doesn't have to shit to do with what I have at home. Hell, she isn't there now. She has been gone since the last time we fucked off. I would have loved to have a child with you. That statement alone should tell you that you are very important to me and not many have a special place in my heart. Hell, I love you girl."

"What about your wife?"
"She is full of shit, and she is not with me."

"L.T. if I had known I would not have done it but I can't undo what is already done."

"Was it a boy? How far along were you?"

"I wasn't far enough to know what the sex was but if I had waited a little longer, I would have known."

"Lizzie you are the first woman to ever get pregnant by me and I always called myself careful."

"It was that night you first took me without a condom, and we made love all night. Do you remember that night?"

I really did remember because I was pissed at Solo, and I forgot to get pick up some and she was out of some. I without a doubt wanted to play roulette and shit got the bitch pregnant. Staring into her warm face I replied, "That is the night I came over here and we fucked all night long. I had stayed out all night and Solo was pissed because I did not tell her where I had been."

"Yeah, that night you got me pregnant, and I didn't know it."

We didn't say anything for a minute. I just held her in my arms as we sat along the bedside. Then Lizzie asked, "You think it's silly of me to be faithful to a man with a wife."

"It is how you feel. Honestly, I do think it's silly to be faithful to a man with a wife. He could never be faithful to you as long as he has someone else. But women do. It's a part of how women are built. They believe if you show a man that you are only with them, they will somehow take the wife's place. Almost all the time that doesn't happen, Lizzie. Men seldom leave home, and women rely on their feelings for him in hopes that he feels the same way but in actuality, you got played. Home is the last thing they leave."

She was quiet for a moment. Lizzie knows that I will be honest to her all she has to do is ask the right questions; which, she never did. Using her weaken voice she spoke almost silently, "We have been messing around for a while, and I don't have any other man but you. I know you are with her, but I somewhat feel that you could leave her one day then see that I have been here for you since day one."

I see now that many outside woman don't understand that we live with a woman and sometimes the shit gets hectic. We will argue with that main woman because we are together. It is then we go to you outside women to have quiet time because at home it's tension. It is never a ploy for you to think we will be with you it is just that we don't want to argue at home.

At home the main woman expects us to pay bills, help with things around the house, if there are children rear them and etc. These main women want a lot out of us so yes, tensions flare and so do words and our tempers, but it is not you we want. With you it is opposite. You may have your own place, make your own money, and so on. You don't really need a lot from us but dick here and there. On the other hand, we don't have reasons to disagree or even get smart because we are not depending on each other for shit. While the main woman, depends on everything from us.

Focusing back to Lizzie, I politely replied, "Babe, who knows what the future holds."

She was fine with that line because she got back into bed and I lay beside her. This time with more shit on my mind because I just found out I could have been a daddy. Before closing my eyes to sleep, I thought *life goes on.*

In my sleep I was talking to Solo, and she was snapping on me. It was unlike her to be talking to me in such a manner. She was saying she going to let God handle me and how I better repent for all I done wrong. My face was unparalleled to her words. It was like my wife was preaching to me before judgment. She continued to go on and on saying, my time is near, and I should have been faithful to her.

Then I saw my grandfather OG Pete. He looked the same as he always did with his favorite suit and tie. While Solo, looked more beautiful than ever. It was like I was sitting there listening to him on one side and Solo on the other. They both were pulling on me to listen to them. Each was making a valid point and I really couldn't decide.

Solo stopped talking. OG Pete, with his cane in his hand repeated a wise saying over and over, *"A burnt child is scared of fire and if you play with fire you will get burned. A burnt child is scared of fire and if you play with fire you will get burned."*

I started hollering no. When I sat up in the bed, Lizzie was screaming. My face was covered in blood from my nose bleeding. Now that shit hasn't happened since Fat Girl days. I in haste went straightway to the bathroom. With Lizzie in tow, she gave me a towel and I held my nose down as I pinched it.

"Oh God, are you ok?"

I waited for my nose to stop bleeding before responding, "Yes."

Lizzie walked out and stared down at the bloody white towel. Then I remembered that I had a nut towel in my pocket and started laughing.

"What is so funny?"

"I thought about how drunk Mudcat got last night and how I dropped him off at this girl house."

"Well, it's nine in the morning, you about to leave?"
"Yeah, I have to go get him."

"You don't want breakfast?"

"No, I will get me something later."

"Ok. Go on and shower while I fix me something."

Lizzie left out to go get my overnight bag out my car trunk. I began to shower. Blood was all on my blue boxers. The water felt great against my skin and the way things were coming at me in my dreams, I needed the water on me. When I came out the shower, she was there wearing a smile. She came over and clung to my damp body saying, "The next time I get pregnant, I won't abort it."

Silly bitch you're a great girl and everything but there won't be a next time. Giving her a light peck on the forehead I spoke, "I know just promise me that you will talk to me about it."

"I will."

She left out. I put on my clean clothes and placed my dirty clothes in the bag. I walked through the kitchen and Lizzie was there reading the paper. I rested my arms around her and spoke as I kissed her, "Girl you mean a lot to me and if I didn't have Solo I would have you, but she is my wife and love her like I love you."

"Solo doesn't know how great of a man she has and when she slips, I will be there to take her place."

"You will take her place?"

"In a heartbeat because I love you more than she ever will."

"Come walk me out."

Lizzie got up and we held hands as we walked to my car. She stood between me and the car saying, "I always hate to see you go. When you going to take me out like you used to?"

"Soon, right now I have a lot going on, got to get this money."

"You always think about money?"

"Try not having it and have to hustle to get every dime you ever had."

She did not respond. Lizzie lifted herself up and kissed me on the lips.

"Now get yo ass in the house before somebody sees my damn meat."

"I'm going, I'm going" she said as she went in the house and shut the door.

I placed my bag in the car and backed out the driveway. Once I got headed to Mudcat, I checked my missed calls and no Solo. I decided to call her.

"Hello."

"Hello my love."

"Hi."

"I miss you."

"I miss you too L. T."

"I dreamed about you and OG Pete again."

The phone was silent. Then Solo spoke, "It's been a while since you actually dreamed about him. What is going on?"

"I dreamed I needed to make a choice between you and him or I believe it was like a choice between you and him. What do you think that means?"

"It sounds like you are going to have to make a great decision in your life."

"How do you and OG Pete play the part?"

"We are the two most important people in your life and we both have a different view point on your life."

"How is that?"

"OG Pete represents everything outside of a marriage while I represent everything within a marriage. It sounds to me that we both want you to follow us you for some reason you can't make up your mind."

I was silent for it made sense. Solo asked, "You there?"

"Yeah, I am. Just thinking about what you said."

"What is your answer?"

"I don't know."

"Babe, one day you will have to know because I don't know is not good enough to make me come home or to keep me at home."

"You right Solo and while you are not here, what kind of picture do you see of me?"

Now she was quiet as she spoke unsurely, "So far, I see a man that loves me but does things to hurt me. I see a man that is painfully afraid to do what is right. The Word of God says when a man leaves his parents and finds a wife, they become one. We supposed to be that oneness, but we have fallen short of that. What you have learned and what you need to learn are colliding. You have to make up your mind."

"I see."

"Is that all you can say?"

"What more do you want me to say?"

"I want you to say that you will become the family man I need you to be or something like that."

"Then that would be your words and not mine. I can't change because you want me too. I have to do it for me."

"I know just don't think I'm going to sit around and wait until you make up your mind about us."

"Solo you are a stepper. Why would I assume anything less?"

"Ok. I'm about to go do some jogging. I love you more than OG Pete and every woman that you have ever known."

Like that she hung up. I know she loves me but a part of me can't help but be who I am. Shrugging off the conversation, I bought my boy and me something to eat at Wendy's and headed towards Dandy's house to pick him up. When I arrived, Mudcat was on the porch. I pulled up and he started walking towards me, "Man hope you have some food. Shit I'm hungry."

"Dandy took her ass somewhere and said I have to wait outside, like I'm going to fucking steal from her broke ass."

"Here man I did think about you and got you something to eat."

"That's what's up."

As he ate, I asked, "How was the pussy last night?"

"Man, she said it was better than before, but I swear, I don't remember getting her guts. I woke up smelling like I fucked but shit I don't remember a damn thing."

"If she says you fucked then you fucked. Be thankful you got a chance to get the pussy again."

"Shit I bought all types of liquor, I tipped my ass off to those bitches and now I don't have shit in my pocket."

"You were the man last night I have to give it to you."

"What did I tell you last night?" Mudcat asked as he drunk some soda.

"About that?"

"Oh, hell what the fuck did I say?"

I laughed then said, "You basically told me that you want connections and your own thing. You also stated that you are the man and how I have it going on."

"Awe Nigga I done told yo ass that sober."

"True but I decided to help you get your own thang today."

"What?"

"You heard me. I am going to let you get your own thang going. I won't give you my all my clients, but I will introduce you to some and it is up to them if they want to trust you."

"L.T. that is some damn good ass news, I am grateful, you hear me? I am very grateful for you helping me."

"Thank me by making it because I don't want to hire yo ass back."

"Man, I won't be coming back. I am going to make it."

"Ok but OG Pete always used to say, a hard head makes a soft ass or if you make your bed hard, you have to lie in it."

"I don't plan on making anything hard because I know how to do everything in the shop."

Women my boy Mudcat is just like a man that wants to be grown but isn't. You women know when men are not doing what they need to be so you give us a rope (let us have space), you sit back (you watch to see what we do; with what you gave us) and we hang ourselves (you tried to tell us the deal but our ego would not allow us to listen; for we think we are grown).

This is my boy, I'm going to let him hang himself because I don't need an inside operator working against me and my empire. I say he is not ready but if he wants to be ready then I'm going to let him get the hell on.

I had Mudcat to show me the building he wants. It is a nice building, but the location is lousy. It has children on every corner and that is a detail that clients look for because with many children around people are always looking for suspicious vehicles. I have already told him this and will not tell him this again. When we got out inspecting the building the police kept traveling back and forth.

That is another no-no. The less the police are around the better, but he likes the place and doesn't seem to want to change his mind. Mudcat said, "They asking one hundred and seventy-five thousand for the half an acre lot, the humongous building and the spacious three-bedroom house."

It puts me in the mind of my old place before I bought the one I have now. The only difference is it's too noticeable. I'm going to try and warn him again, so I said, "I like it but it is not what you need. The police come by and too many families on the strip and that mean nosey neighbors."

"Man, you always rain on my parade. Be happy for me. Just admit it is better than yours?"

I can't believe he said that. Again, as nicely as I could, I said "I am happy for you but if you want it go for it. Go for it but I tried telling you."

"I don't have all the money."

"How much do you have?"

"Only one hundred and seventy-five thousand dollars."

"So, you need one hundred thousand more bing-bings?"

"Yeah, I need those bing-bing dollars, but I understand if you can't help me."

"It's not that I can't help you. The question is how are you going to pay back?"

"Do you know how long it would take me to pay that back?"

"I will front the money and almost all you make goes back to me for repayment."

"What do you mean?"

"If you make ten thousand, I get seven."

"That means I have to have a lot of fucking money rolling in."

"That's on you and how you make it."

"Bet."

"Get the legal paperwork, and I will have my lawyer look them over."

"You act like you don't trust me. It's not that but this is a business, and it must be handled as a business transaction."

"Yeah, you right L. T."

We left and I dropped him off at his crib. I told him that he no longer have to come in but to let me know when the papers were ready. As I went on to my shop, I had to check things out and everything was still in place as I suspected. I got a few more calls to for some more money to roll in and that pleased me. Then I remembered that today was the day I am to have dinner with Monica and her children. I went and showered and put on something simple.

CHAPTER 10

It is always a pleasure to see the children. They are well groomed children that are polite and love their mom. I always try to bring them something as a reward for being good and it always work. When I called her, I told her I was on my way and she sounded just as excited as the children. My first stop was to the toy and candy shop. I always bring them gummy worms and doughnuts of all kinds and a toy each. For Monica, I got flowers.

I didn't get a chance to get out the car for they were all over me. She had to come to the car and get the children. I can tell she was nervous and half ashamed because of the way they were acting. It made me feel good on the inside to know that they really liked me; even for my gifts. I got out the car and spoke, "Calm down and let me get a chance to make it inside."

They were all over me screaming, hi Mr. L. T. and where the snacks. Once they settled, they went inside. I took a better look at her. Her pretty dark skin was flawless and shiny. Her dress was nice and short but presentable for the presence of a man. The way her hair made her eyes look, I wanted to bypass what she has to do and go straight to bed. Blushing she dropped her head to say, "I am so sorry they are acting like this."

Lifting up her head to speak to her mind and heart, I said, "They are children, and I love them as if they were my own. I'm glad they want to come to me."

She would not say a word. I then spoke, "These are for you, and the other things are for the children."

Monica took the flowers and buried her nose and face into their fragrance. Lifting up her eyes just enough to meet my eyes, she asked "How did you know I love these flowers?"

"I'm a man and it's my business to know what type of things a woman in my life likes."

"Why do you have to be so good to me and the children?"

"I am only being me and if that means being good to you all then that is what I do. I can't help it if I see a great woman in front of me that needs someone to be there for her and her children."

I saw her toddler come outside so I leaned closer breathed into her ear, to impregnate her mind by sexually transmitting the words, "Above all you look beautiful, good enough to eat."

Removing my mouth from her ear so my mouth could make a kiss loud enough for her to hear but close enough to see. She smiled and really began to blush. Her child tugged on her leg, and she picked him up.

Always remember that the majority women go by what they hear and that is why you can be an ugly man but if you have a good conversation mouth piece, you can make the prettiest girl fall for you. It is how you use your words and how romantic you sound. Men on the other hand; go by what they see. That is why it is important to a woman that she looks good, show some breast prints, reveal legs and have your hair fix. If your face is off, the rest of you must be on point.

As for men, we love to look at the woman and that plays images in our mind about how you would feel. We don't too much give a damn how soft your voice is, it is how you look and smell (it's a package). Being that she heard me speak on eating her she is having that on her mind and every time she looks at me I will lick my lips as if I don't know what I am doing. I have to keep sex on her mind if I want that ass tonight.

The three of us walked inside and the children were sitting on the couch waiting on us. When I walked in, they bomb rushed me with their hugs. It felt nice to feel love from innocent children and that is why I'm seriously considering Solo's proposal.

"Your mother has your gifts."

"Which none of you will get until we have eaten."

Her daughter said, "Let us eat so we can get our gifts."

"Your mom will give you all your gifts soon. Lets' go to the table."

The kids obeyed me, and I know she is impressed by the way I handle the children. I wasn't too impressed because it is something about the sight of a man or father figure that makes children line up. The children and I sat at the table while Monica fixed the plates. Once she sat the food on the table everyone held hands. I of course held Monica's and every chance I could I would touch her. *Remember this is the foreplay the build-up of what is to come.*

With each touch she would swallow hard. I could tell that no man has ever done this to her before and I am taking pleasure to be her first. We all began to eat.

"I haven't had a home cooked meal in a very long time."

"You haven't?"

"No, I haven't."

"Then we must cook for you more often."

"Yes, you should" I spoke as I licked my lips.

I turned my eyes toward her. She was indeed looking but when she saw me, she turned her head. As the dinner progressed, it was great. In reality, it was wonderful to have the feel of a family and I like it. The children were being children and when they would argue I would put it to a halt quickly and Monica admired that.

Every chance I got I was touching her lightly and licking my lips. The way she was watching me, I knew it was working. I even went as far as licking my tongue out at her to entice her and she could only shake her head. I was on a roll with her, and I really liked it. I never thought about my own situation. My brain would not let anything else process but what I was feeling right now, with her.

After supper we all ate pecan pie. It was store bought but it still was delicious. The entire family atmosphere was great. There was always something going on and the way she would take charge when they got out of hand was great. It was like the God Solo was telling me about was showing me what a family life would look like and I liked the picture. I had always looked on my own childhood and never had the philosophy of the American family to enter my mind.

"What are your thoughts?" Monica asked as she touched my hand.

"It is the idea of having a family and how just being here brings me a sense of peace."

"Children are a blessing from God and I love them all."

"I can tell."

Interrupting our moment where the children. They all came to say good night to me and to their mother. The one next to the toddler asked me to read him a story. I was flabbergasted that a child wanted me to perform such act. They child showed me to the room he shared with his brother. He handed me the book "The Three Little Pigs." Both of the boys snuggled into bed and listened to me reenact the story. This is the first time in my life that I actually felt important.

Money, women and my wife are good things but to be idolized in the eyes of a child means more. After I finished reading, they were asleep. I put the book back on their shelf, turned off the light and eased the door closed. When I made it downstairs the house was quiet except for a little Keith Sweat playing. That kind of music means sex, but I won't take her, not just yet. She must continue to think it is not about the sex.

I looked to my left and there was Monica. She had on a two-piece night set and it was a fucking turn on. Smiling I walked over and I heard her say, "I freshened up while you were reading to the boys."

"You still look great."
"Come sit with me. I want to talk to you."

Just like a damn woman, wanting to talk with her lips when I can think of other body parts and a pair of balls that wants to be in the conversation. She patted on the love seat for me to come and I did. As I sat down, her right arm was on the back of the seat with her left hand holding the other hand; while, one leg was perched up and the other one dangled towards the floor without touching it. *Just right for the picking,* I thought as I sat beside her and engulfed her erotic scent to my nostrils.

"Tonight, I want to know about the real L.T."

She threw me a curve ball. My mind went blank and wondered *what the hell she talking about?* Gathering my words I took a finger and made circles to trace her knee as I spoke, "Don't ask a question if you are not prepared for the answer."

"I am prepared for any answer you give me."

"What answers are you seeking?"

"I seek any answer you are willing to tell me."

"What is it that you really want to know?"

"For starters I know you are married."

You talk about putting water on a fire. Talk about a man's wife while he is trying to fuck you, I guarantee that is a showstopper. I cut in to say, "Yes I am married."

"Are you happy?"

"Why wouldn't I be?"

"You can't be, if you are here with me."

"Not true."

"Ok. Can your wife be like this with another man and still love you?"

"She can but she isn't like that. It's not to say she won't mess up but what do you really want to know about my marriage."

"What has driven you to having an affair? I mean you claim you love her?"

"Yes, I love her dearly and would not change anything for her but what love has to do with it?"
"We women, tend to feel that if a man cheats then he must not really love the one he cheated on. How can you explain the meaning of this so called love?"

Making sure to choose my words carefully, I spoke with seriousness, "I can only speak from my point of view. Love and sex are two different things. Love is to the one you give your heart too and sex is just the motion of getting your dick wet or getting that nut. I don't confuse the two because if you do then you will get in a mess, and somebody will fall in love."

"But love goes with sex and sex with love. You can't have one without the other."

"Not so. Men are wired differently than women and what you call love, we call care. What you call making love, we call fucking."

"So, you care about the outside woman?"

"I wouldn't say that and what do you mean outside women?"

"We are grown, and I know like you know that I am not your only, first indiscretions for that matter. Are you a habitual cheater?"

"I have friends if that is what you want to know, and anything can be a habit. You are the only friend I have right now, if you must know."

"Am I really?"

"Really, you are the only one I see now?"

"Where do I play into all of this? I mean I have kids, and I need someone that can help me."

"Depends what you call this?"

"I mean what we have going on?"

"Depends on what you call, what we have going on?"

"You always answer a question with a question?"

"Do you always ask questions you already know the answer too?"

Monica looked away with a smile as she said, "I guess you have it all mapped out."

I touched her hand and replied, "I do to a degree, but I never counted on you and your children to be a wonderful as you all are and that is real. There is something about you."

"We have never counted on meeting you and have you to be such the man you are and what is it about me?"

"You are to me one of a kind and from the first time I came into this house, I could feel the love that you have here. It's the kind of love that I never received as a child. Call it weird if you want but I felt that and that made me want you even more."

"It does?"

"Yes, it does but kind of man do you take me to be?"

"The just the man that will break my heart but make me feel special. You are the kind of man that has a way of making a woman go against all she knows just to be with you. To me you are perfect."

Monica touched me to say, "I know I can't replace your wife but if given half the chance I know you can be happy with me but if you are cheating on her with me, you will cheat on me with someone else. I just don't know if I want to lose my heart again but this time to a married man."

"You are the first woman that I have ever sat down and talked to; especially talking about my life and my wife. Fate has a way of playing in our lives. Maybe it is just that?"

"Just what?"

"Fate that we are here sharing this time together, but it is funny that I am here with you and not trying to work things out with my wife."

"You want her to come back home?"

"I don't know. She left me and evidently there she must have reasons to leave."

"I can't picture you being a bad husband to her."

"I spend a lot of time in the streets making money for the house, providing this and that. I don't curse her out and I don't beat on her verbally or physically."

"Maybe you not being with her, is why you two fell apart?"

"Maybe but right now, I wouldn't trade this time with you for anything, and I mean that."

"Stop it before you have to give into account."

"Give into account on how I feel or what I feel like doing right now?"
"Either or."

The moment was perfect as we each leaned into a kiss. Her lips were softer than before. It never occurred to me that a top pair of lips would taste so saccharine with sweet sugar. The more we kissed the feverish I was feeling for her. I never knew a kiss would be that good. Before I knew it my hands were all over her and touching all her curvy love handles. Every ripple my hands went over happened to bring me closer to the bank of her goodness.

Monica short ass fits my tall body flawlessly. Every single move I took was timed to perfection with her and at this point we were lying on the couch corner just kissing.

"Wait, L. T."

I removed my lips from hers to say nothing for my eyes and my breathing were telling her all I couldn't say but she did say, "I want you to know that I am thankful for the time you spend with me and my children, predominantly me. The designs of how a father is to interact with his family and treat his wife means more than you will ever know. Even though, it is not right for you to be here, but God knows I need you here. I needed to come alive, and I needed to think that a man can find me attractive. You did all that. I've never fondled the thought of being involved since my husband left but you brought something unique and tangible. With all that being said, it would give me great honor if I can have you tonight."

I was blown away and ready. She stopped the flow to spill out her damn feelings. *Anything for a nut* I thought as I kissed her with more passion. This time she took me by the hand, and we went upstairs to her bedroom door. We paused and she whispered, "I've never had a man other than my husband in this bed in this house for that matter."

Being romantic, I opened the bedroom door to a dim room as I lifted her up as if she were my bride. With joy she covered my neck with her arms as I walked into the room and closing the door with my foot. I could only stare at her as I securely lay her on the plush king-size bed. I began to be lost in her as I resumed the kissing. She was in return just as heated up as I. In all my days I never felt so spun out of control over any woman.

The sensation that accompanied me led to the valley beneath her stomach. The second my mouth came into contact with her breast the door busted open. It was her son, and he was crying. I presume from a bad dream. However, we both jolted up. She ran over to him and coherence him back to bed.

While she was gone, I decided that I better stick to the game plan and not deviate. I was still dressed and that was good now it was time for me to leave. When she came back, she saw me standing and looking out the window. I heard the door lock behind her as she spoke using a raspy tone, "Are you leaving?"

Without facing her I said, "Yes, if your son had not disrupted us, I would have lost myself in your loving and enjoyed it too much. I hadn't had a woman since I been with you. I haven't even had my wife and all I want and crave is you and what you can give me."

"I am in dire need of you and wish you would reconsider. Tonight, it will be just for us. We can be together whenever we need some loving."

"If that is the case, I am going to want you every night and every waking moment I live."

Facing her now, I could see her nipples harden from the outfit. *Such a turn on* I thought as I spoke, "It may be best if I leave."

"Please don't leave me in this condition."

Seeing the pain of me leaving in her eyes, didn't do anything for me. I spoke as I could and said, "I don't want you to be hurt in my affair because I love my wife and I don't plan to leave her. She may leave me, but I won't leave her. I can't in good conscious do this to you. If I were a dog ass Nigga I wouldn't care less but when a woman's feelings are involved a man must tread lightly."

"I understand but will you promise that you will think about me and the offer I have for you?"

"Monica I will always think about you offer or not. I am already regretting leaving you tonight, but I can't make a sound decision if I am thinking with my dick, now can I?"

She didn't answer at first. When she lay on the bed she spoke with her legs open, "No you can't but the way I am feeling, use me. I don't care you have a wife all I need is to be with a man that wants me."

In this condition, women don't know what they ask for. They think they want a man to have them for a few minutes, and they will feel better, but they won't because the more they are with that man, the more they have to have that man. Sure, a dog ass Nigga like me is going to fuck her. I needed her think that my dick has a conscious. She fell for the "I have to do what is right theory."

Taking off my shoes and disrobing my clothes, I placed myself next to her and spoke, "I don't want you to regret making love to another woman's husband and hate me in the process. I don't want you to fuck at the spare of the moment. You don't owe anything. I want you to want me because you want me."

"Right now, you are not her husband, you are my man. I will not regret you taking me the way I need to be taken."

Trying not to be impatient but playing this "I really don't want it game" has taken its toll. I was all over Monica as she lay in the middle of the bed. Skipping all that kissing and arousal game, I went in for the kill. Balancing myself on my left elbow I lifted up and inserted my friend into her friend. I almost shouted.

It gave me the feeling of eating ice cream on a hot day. That is just how it was to be inside her.

The first twist of my hips caused me to feel faint because it was just that damn good. Her pussy made me feel the way Superman is to kryptonite. The pussy was nice fitting on every angle. It was not loose or too tight but deep enough for me to lose control. No problem ever arose, if it were one it dissipated as she elevated her hips to meet my thrusting. Her short fat ass was throwing her pussy from every direction as she allowed me to find comfort in her body. I never dreamed that getting on top of her would be this powerful or this intimate, but it was. I could not think straight, and I did not want to think straight.

Monica's loving was way strange. The last time I fucked her, I was rough housing her ass and she allowed me to have my way. This new way is awesome, but it is scary mainly for the way she was rocking her body with my rhythm. That mattered not for I was in control. The method she was using to keep calm was not working. She was crying out for more as I stayed on her and gave her the dick she deserved.

I could not believe how incredible and unpredictable the moment was for me. Though, she was under me and throwing her pussy back to me, I could feel the intensity of our body's language. This woman beneath me began to claw at my back as she begun to peak. I being a man sped up the process by crushing my body into hers faster and faster until, I too cried out.

For the first time in a long time, I did not trust myself to move. I finally found a piece of ass that had me craving it. The pussy is a high mark but not good enough. I knew her eyes were closed for she was making love like the rest of the women, I fuck. When she did look at me, she said, "I was making love, wasn't I?"

"You were taking care of a man that really needed to release himself."

"I was making love, wasn't I?"

Knowing that I must tell her I spoke, "Yes, you were and that is what I was afraid of and that is you falling for a man like me."

"I don't mind being the other woman, I just want to be the only outside woman. I don't believe I can fuck without feelings."

"I know you can't because you are a woman."

I eased up off her and lay on my back. My dick was sticking to my leg and shit, and I could not help but look at her. *If his dick sticks to his leg, it is a sign that he fucked good. If it has a little life, you have to try it again.* Giving my attention back to Monica, she is short and fat but she is worth seeing. Her attitude is on great and her idealism of family is on point. You can't help it but want her.

We did not wipe off or anything. I turned over and watch her sleep soundly. I closed my eyes and all I could see was my life. It took me back to when I was provoked to hit my mother and how she and I fought. I even saw how I learned that I have a way with words, and I used its full potential. Most of all I saw my boy Mudcat and how he hated on me. I opened my eyes and saw I was still at Monica's. I pulled her close to me and held her as she slept.

When I opened my eyes, it was morning, and she was not in bed. I got up and looked at my cell phone. I saw that Dandy and Mudcat called. "I'm not going to call them back just yet" I said as I sat on side the bed.

Before I realized it, I yelled out loud enough for the sound to reach my ears, "Damn! Last night was the first time I honestly fucked without getting my dick sucked." Her pussy must be good?"

"I thought you were up."

She looked beautiful, secretive and sexy. Monica walked over to me and continued speaking, "I'm cooking breakfast, I know you are hungry."

"Not really but where are your children?"

"They are still asleep. Why?"

"Good, I want to shower and if you don't mind, please get my bag from out my car."

I gave her the keys, and she left out. When she returned, she handed my bag as I spoke, "Thank you."

"You are welcomed."

I opened my bag and took out my own towel, soap and a new set of clothes.

"You come prepared, don't you?"

"I always have extra clothes because you never know when you need to put on something else."

With humor in her tone Monica said, "That sounds like what I do for my children."

"Pretty much."
"You ok? You seem distant this morning?"

"I'm ok. Why you ask?"

"You don't have any regrets, do you?"

"No, should I?"

"No but I can tell that you are not the same man."

She left out and I stepped in the shower. I closed my eyes as I lathered up my body. No matter how tight they were closed the sex of last night was presently with me. To erase the images of her, moving my head back and forth became the option. That was not enough. The look on her face could not be avoided as I drilled her none-stop.

The more I placed my hands on my face the more Monica's face penetrated my mind. Therefore, I decided to position my body to the back of the shower. This direction proved to be an injustice. The warm water race down my back and at that I remembered all too well the last time we were in her shower. Literally the manifestation of us against the wall came into play.

There we were in the shower fucking. You could tell that I was engrossed in the task because my muscles flexing in my back. Above all, it is her that my eyes saw. Her soaked dark skin, and puffy lips and the way her mouth would open to say ouch as I buried myself inside her continuously. *Oh what a believable feeling* I thought as I smiled at the memory. I could not help but grin as those snuggly visions that crossed my mind of my night with Monica emerged.

Stepping out the shower, I dried off and put on the clean clothes. I wanted to be finished before the children woke up because I am not their father and I know what this could look like to a child. That all changed once I started out the bedroom door. Her son was there. With one blanket in his hand and his shirt in his mouth he spoke between clenched teeth saying, "Da-Da?"

I didn't know what to say for I know what he means because a man is in the home with his mom and his real dad is not present. There is only explanation and that is the one word he said. Plainly, as I could I spoke, "No, Mr."

He turned around and left out the door. I went down the steps and saw Monica. I smiled and said, "Beautiful, your son said da-da."

Her mouth fell open and asked, "What you tell him, L. T.?"

"I said no, Mr."

"I'm so sorry my son said that. He has never seen any other man except his father with me."
"Don't apologize. He is a child. He only knows what he sees and that is a man that is not his father, being with his mother. He sees me with you and how you smile. He knows but does not understand."

Monica did not say another word. I went over to her and pecked her cheek and that too smelled damn good. She asked before I got ready to leave, "When will I see you?"

"I don't know."

"Was it that bad?"

"OH NO! It was damn good and shit you put something on my mind. I have to prioritize."

"You really are saying that it is going to be a while before we see each other?"

"I can't say that. Just know that if you don't see me I am not with anyone. I'm going to be on that money like never before. I may come up for air then again, I may not. I will be the only one in my shop, so I won't be able to be as free as I used to be. Feel free to call me or leave a message. If possible, I will check it and call you back but starting today I go to do what I got to do."

"I see."

"Here."

She looked at the money and said, "What you think you are paying for my services?"

"No, you don't have to ever fuck me, if you don't want too because this is not for that. It is something I want you and the children to have. As for your services, I don't pay for pussy. Never have, never will."

"I'm sorry it's just that, the idea was the first thing to cross my mind."

"It's ok. It is a normal reaction, and I understand but this is money I got, and it is for you all. Take it."

Monica took the money and gave me a big hug to say, "Your wife should be very happy to have your love."

"She should be but she doesn't appreciate me like you do."

I opened the front door and left out.

CHAPTER 11

I got in my car to leave. I was hungry but not really for the little boy gave me something to think about. Not letting it register that I am trying to play daddy to some children that are in need of a father, I kept driving. Soon as I got it home, I went to the shop. For the first time, my wife crossed my mind. Making up my mind to call her, I went in the shop office and dialed her number. Soon as I was about to hang up she picked up and said, "Hi."

Her voice sounded pleasant, and I never thought about how much I miss talking to her until now. I was having the feeling of missing everything about her, I mean everything. Determined to go straight into the reason I spoke without guarantee on how she would react, "You crossed my mind, and I just wanted to hear your voice."

"Ok."

There was a long pause because she sounded changed, in some way. I stated, "Why the short answers?"

"No reason."

"Solo we have been married for a minute and together even longer. I know you like you know me. Out with it."

"Are you ready to do as I asked? Are you ready for us to be a legal family?"

"That is getting old. You come at me with the same thing."

"L. T. I come at you with the same thing because you keep giving me the same answers. Change your answers."

"I can't promise that. I can however promise to love you everything else is up for grabs. It's up to you if you want to be here with me or not."

"Up to me? I left you in hopes to better you and us."

"You don't want to leave me. I can break you down and call it the day and won't think anything else about you; in fact, you're a will be an afterthought and can be replaced- just like that"
"I can be replaced?"

"Isn't that what I said?"

"I got out of your way so you can find your way. I believe that if I am not with you, you can do what you need to do on your own without me there to influence your behavior but it seem to have backfired."

"What do you mean you got out of my way?"

"It should have occurred to you that I haven't been in contact with you, but it hasn't. I'm not coming to the house for anything, and you still don't get it. You don't realize how much having you is important to me. I never cared for the money or this lifestyle. I wouldn't care if you never make millions, thousands for that. I only want you. No amount of money can be out on my love for you. I simply can't be bought."

"No one is trying to buy you, but everything has a price, and every limit has a boundary."

"You may buy yourself in that bed or lie yourself in another one, but I can't have you if they all have you too. You can't be faithful to me and faithful to everything else. Something comes up short and I fear it's our marriage."

"Our marriage will be just fine if you do you and let me do me. But you try to live my life and yours too. Damn babe, I'm a man and I know these streets. Go save your own soul."

"It sounds like they all win."

"Who are they?"

"They all include everyone but me. There's Mudcat, your clients, your shop and don't let me forget the money you love to make. Anything outside of me is they all. You want to have your cake and eat it too. You can't do that. Now it's time out for being greedy."

"All I do is for us and only us. You mean everything to me, but you don't understand me like the streets."

"How can I mean everything to you, and everything is important to you but me. Do you not care about how I feel? Has it not registered that you are the perfect man to everyone but me? I thought that by me leaving you, you could think clearly but it has only turned you worse. You don't really think about me. You think about everything but me."

"That's not true. I think about you but right about now you fucking up a dream."

The line was silent. To break the silence she said, "You only think about me when you haven't heard from me in a while or if you messing around because you and I both know you would have sex before you beat your meat. You haven't slept with me in a while, so who you screwing?"

"You have left me, and you want to know what I'm doing. I'm not doing anything you aren't doing. Now who are you screwing?"

"Rest assure, whatever I am doing, sexing is not one of them. I want my marriage, but I can't want my marriage alone. It's like you don't want my direction or my input on how things should go. I understand that you are the almighty Lamar Times but you are my husband also. You are being faithful to everyone but me. If I need time with you, I better be talking about money, if I'm not I better wait until you nut. Do you not care that I am not with you? Do you not care that I am doing this for us?"

"For us, you the one who left us, and I don't' need another motherfucker trying to guide me. These streets have taught me that if I don't get it then I won't have it. They have been here for me when you weren't. There have been times when you left me alone. So yeah, the streets are my bitch, and I enjoy fucking her because the pussy is good. I love what she gives me head, and I know she is there for me. You ran off and left me to defend what we have alone. You fucking left me. Then you want to talk about our marriage this and that. What about me and my marriage to streets?"

"If you want those streets and not do what is right for me? Then you married to the wrong one."

Solo hung up. I started talking out, "Damn she done got me out my zone. Fuck! Bitch! Damn bitch!"

Women must understand that in some cases, the streets is where a man feels the love he doesn't get at home. The streets share what they have, not like some church folks. A drunk will give you a swallow of their liquor quicker than a church person will feed you a meal. People in the street will not talk about you but a church person will. The streets will give you want you need; love, sex, money, time and space; while, a church person will give it with a catch behind it. Church people will get mad if you don't go to church; while, the streets say that you have God in you.

Solo is like many women. When they change they want everything around them to change. Not so. Men are often hardheaded and it takes traumatic experience before we come around; it's just how it is as a man. We have our God in the streets because if you place a sack of potatoes and a salad in front of a hungry man; which you think he will choose? The sack of potatoes because with those potatoes he can bake them, boil them, fry them or grill them; with the salad nothing but plainly eat it.

Closing my thoughts of my wife, I took in a sigh and left out. I began doing work Mudcat normally would do. Luckily, I knew how to do all this before he came on the scene. I began to throw myself into my work. In fact, I will save thousands of dollars more by doing it myself and I get the job done more effectively. Its' not to say that he won't do great work; he does quality work at a slower rate. During this time of the year scrapping is at an all-time high and I need the parts taken down more faster than ever.

The weeks seem to roll by like water in a river and before I knew it two months were gone unnoticed. I had been living and breathing my shop. I didn't care to talk to anyone, not even my wife. In fact, it bothered me not because she said her say the last time I talked to her. I would check my messages and not return any calls for my mind was on that paper and not on pussy. If I allowed myself to lose sight of the big picture of making that money, than pussy would rule me. *Pussy can be a distraction. It is one of the biggest mistake men make, they hustle behind pussy but if you hustle behind money, pussy will come with it.*

After my last client left, I saw five miss calls from Dandy. *Why she calling me? I haven't been fucking off with her or anyone* I thought. I almost called her back but she rang me first. I answered, "What is it?"

"What the fuck been going on with yo ass? You done put a bitch down and shit?"

"Dandy I've been busy."

"I know yo ass been busy cuz I been calling yo ass. I started to come by but didn't know what the deal was wit yo ass."

"I'm good. What's up?"

"Nothing, you just need to learn to check yo fucking cell phone. The bitch was going to voicemail for weeks now."

"You have me on the phone now, what is wrong?"

"I hear yo ass got another piece of ass."

"Yes, her name is Solo, my wife but other than her my shop."

"Yo ass knows what the hell I am talking about."

"Look, I have my wife Solo, and I don't know why you are calling me accusing me of women. If you aren't having a problem with your property or problem with a vehicle, then you don't need to call me about nonsense. Do like you have been doing and that is mailing your payments. I'm not in the mood for shit. I am on that paper chase."

I hung up on Dandy because now some bitch is talking, and you never underestimate a bitch mainly if she has been or is hurt. You always play it safe, and you keep your cool at all times. If you are angry you can't think straight. Regardless of what Dandy was saying I was determined to down play it and keep on stepping.

It's when you aren't doing shit, when your shit comes out but as long as you are doing shit, no one knows shit. As for mentioning your wife's name you always talk in a mist. Bitches will try to set you up by calling you and having another bitch on the line for proof. Little do they know is, if you get caught up, you can still fuck both of them especially if the dick is good. They will think they have done something if they hear you say words or think they have you cornered, when in reality they only make your game more popular.

Smiling I knew someone was on the line or something was going on because Dandy never calls me like that. She knows too well that I don't discuss shit like that on the phone. I do that shit in person. For her to say I have another piece of ass, someone thinks I am spending time somewhere, other than at my shop. *Bitches always hating* I thought as I forgot all about Dandy's phone call.

At night, when I got lonely, I went to my shop to work. I am more determined than ever to make this money because I promised myself a long time ago that I would not go hungry as long as I can hustle. I began to work even harder on the upcoming paint job in the back room. My business is thriving better than ever, and I have more than enough money to quit but the more I make the more I have to have.

Soon as I came up for air, the time was seven thirty am. It was time for the shop to open. Low and behold, I saw my boy Mudcat standing in the front door. I spoke as we greeted each other with our familiar handshake, "Dammit boy! What the hell blew your "I want my own thang ass" back here?"

"Shit I haven't heard from you and the bitches haven't heard from you, so I came to go see what the hell is up with yo ass."

"Shit working and working, and getting that paper."

"I feel ya on that my Nigga."

"How is your shop going?"

"It's not going. The shit isn't going anywhere but down a fucking drain."

"What the hell happened for it to go down the drain?"

"Business really slow. Other than my location, police and children, it seems that they don't want me without you."

"I tried to tell you that, but you wouldn't listen, so I said fuck it, you grown."

"Man, I was letting pussy guide me and that bitch led me in a ditch. My ass is in a hole, and I can't get out. I'm asking you as a friend to buy me out. Take all the profits and hire me back."
"This woman friend of yours; where she fits into all this?"

"Her ass doesn't. I haven't heard from her and when I did she told me she was pregnant, and I only fucked her once and at that I didn't remember getting it."

"How the hell you didn't remember getting it?"

"Shit with an ass like that, you would think I would remember. But her ass said it's a good chance that it is mine."

"You about to be a daddy? I can't believe this."

"Me either. I might be a dead ass daddy because her man is going to hit the damn roof."

"Not if he's fucking her."

"True but her ass won't tell me shit."

"Well, is she going to tell him?"

"No, she going to play it off as his and now I have to sell all I have."

"Why the fuck you have to sell all you have?"

"Because the devious, deceitful, sneaky, double crossing ass bitch wants to take me for everything I have. So, if I don't have anything, her dirty ass can't take anything."

I waited a few minutes to him. He is my boy, but the fact remains that he told me what he thought about me that night. I haven't quite forgotten that. He then said, "L. T. we have been through so much and I really need your help. I tried and failed. I want to come back and work with you and for you. I've made mistakes and some mistakes I allowed the wrong head to guide me. But bitches can be so bitter and mean they would use you in their scheme. I really thought she was different."

"After all the bitches you knew me to fuck off with, you just now realizing how a bitch can be?"

"Hell yeah, the bitch took my heart down through there, brought it back and stomped on that bitch. So, what you say? Can ya boy come back and work like never before?"

I paused to make him think that I was uncertain of his loyalty and friendship. Looking at him, I didn't feel sorry for him so I spoke, "Because you have been the best investment I have ever made, you can come on back."

Never in my days have I seen Mudcat so proud. It was so unlike him to show any joy except about women. However, today he was exceedingly happy as he proclaimed, "Man you don't know how much this shit means to me. I can start right now if you want."

"I need the break. Let's go to my Lawyers office and have things done the right way."

Mudcat and I went to my Lawyers office. She had the papers drawn up as we waited. It was almost pleasing to have him back, but I wasn't ecstatic as I should be. Something was hazy and he was too eager to come back to work; then again, I haven't talked to people outside of my clients in a while.

We came back to the shop and Mudcat went straight to work. I went in the office to rest for it was odd to be in here and not in the shop. I listened to some of my messages, and one was from Lizzie. She was saying that she was tired of waiting on me and this was her last month living at the property. Lizzie also said she would be gone by the end of the month and for me to leave her alone and not look her up.

I hope she don't think that I would come after her because I don't chase pussy. Then again, she has done me a favor. It saved me the time to put her ass down. She just doesn't know that pussy comes at a man, on a daily basis and for her to leave only opens opportunities for me.

Honestly, Monica had been crossing my mind, and I wanted to go see her but didn't want to do more damage to her than I already have. Most of all it is her loving that I miss. The last time I we slept together, her pussy put some heavy shit on my mind. For days, I could only think about her, and I never think about bitches like that. Somehow, Monica was different, and I like different.

The thrill of wanting some pussy came over me. Shaking the fuck feeling off me, I went back to work with Mudcat. He was working harder than ever, and he wasn't riding the clock like use to; which was an improvement. When lunch time came, we took a break in my office. We ate sandwiches and discussed what's been going on.

From his speech, I could tell that he was indeed a better man, and I hated that it took pussy to get him to grow up but it did. He was optimistic about learning how to save his money and better himself. Mudcat told me that he has been slowing off the drink but still love the hoes. I could only laugh because deep down inside he was the same boy.

I did not know that I missed talking to him and it wasn't because he has been my only company. He really spoke as if he was happy to be back here working and part of me believed him. Whenever I would mention his old girl, he would tense up as if she was a sore subject and I would let it ride. For if I know one thing, I know he will tell me how she played him and betrayed him at the same time.

It got close to quitting time, and I didn't want to ask but I did anyway, "Was it hard for you to come back and ask me for your old job back?"

He stared at me then said, "Man it was harder than you can ever know. Being that I am here I have the notion that I am inadequate as a man because I failed. I know that you would let me come back because of my work history and because the level of work I do. I'm just thrilled you gave me another chance, and I want to tell you that I am sorry for all the wrong and harm that I did to you. I can't take back for what happened I can only go from this point on."

"Mudcat, apology accepted and you still my number one boy."

"That means a lot to me to hear you think of me in that fashion. I love you man."

"Likewise here, likewise here."

Mudcat has always been the closer thing to a brother that I ever known. Some of it is why I trust him because I have known him for so many years. Since the day I put him on, we have been like two peas in a pot, thicker than thieves and closer than any other human in my life. I have been through so much shit with him and to see him like this and to know how he was feeling did a toll on my mind. Never would I think that he was feeling like that towards me, when I have done everything in my power to rise so we both could rise.

Now he is here in need of help and I as usual offered my assistance to him. I was truly pleased that he came to me and that I could help him. I felt pretty good knowing that he is going to be alright. I am just thrilled to have my number one boy back on my team. Mudcat left and I went in the house.

When I walked in, I for the first time sensed the loneliness and bareness. It was unlike Monica's house when I was last over there, and the children were making things alive. It was always something going on and it was like me wishing that was my life, my happy childhood life. I went in the bathroom and took a shower and hated it.

I was alone and men don't like to be alone. I speedily finished my shower and placed a towel around me. I got in bed and thought about Monica. Before I knew what I was doing, I called her. The phone rung and rung; thinking she might be asleep, I hung up. Making the ceiling my focal point, I stared and stared until the sound of my cell ringing disturbed me.

"Hello."

"Hi stranger."

I removed the phone from my ear to see that Monica did without a doubt call me back.

"How you been?"

"I've been good and what about yourself?"

"Working hard. How are the children?"

"They good as well. I must acknowledge I am weary that you are calling me."

"Why would you think that?"

"I haven't heard from you since the last time you were at my house and that has been weeks ago. You haven't called, text and you haven't even checked to see if we were alive."

"Monica, I apologize. I haven't been talking or seeing anyone. Since the day I left you, I have hidden myself in my work."

The line was quiet. To break the awkwardness, I spoke, "I've missed you."

"I can't lie I miss you too."

"Will I ever be able to make it up to you and the children?"

"You can."

"Ok."

"Is that all you can say?"

"Yeah, to be honest, my boy came over and started back working with me and he is the first person outside of work that I have talked to. You are the second. I haven't even talked to my wife."

"Do you want to talk to her?"

"No not really because she makes her point clear when I last talked to her. I am not in the mood to have history repeat itself."

"I see."

"Yup."
We got quiet for a few more seconds before she said, "I've been having time to think about us and whatever this is we call ourselves having."

"What you come up with?"

"I came up with the concept that I was not important enough for you to be with."
"You came up with that all by yourself?"

"Yes, and it hurt. You weren't here for me to talk to and I didn't know what to do. I didn't know if your wife came back or what."

"She's still gone."

"I know that now but then there was no idea. You just quit talking to me and you left me hanging. It wasn't right."

"What if I were back to my wife, then what?"

"Then you are back with your wife, simple as that. I can't change it but she is your wife, and I am just a friend with benefits."

"Don't say you are just a friend. You have a little weight, with your short fat ass."

She laughed her hearty laugh, and I liked it. Monica sounded happy.

"You happy?" Monica asked as the laughter died down.

"Are you happy?" She questioned me back.

"Depends on what you call happy?"

"It is whatever you call it."

"Well money can't make you happy like having someone to love could then again what is love?"

"Here you go with all those questions for answers" Monica said as she laughed.

"You haven't changed. Will you ever change?"

It was something about that inquiry that puzzled me. Only my wife ever stated anything about change and me in the same sentence.

"Beautiful, I have had a long day, and I really need to rest. I felt the need to call you because I walked into my house tonight and it didn't feel anything like your home."

"Home is where the heart is and it depends on where you call home. Good night L.T. I must chat with you soon. There are some things I need to tell you."

Monica got off the phone and I was somewhat gland because now I am thinking of my wife and how the hell am I going to fix whatever she claims is broken. Or do I need to see if Monica is the flavor for me to have? I am at a crossroad in my life. I am at a place where money rules and money can do anything and everything but make you healthy and keep you happy.

"Have I ever been happy?"

I questioned myself. Thinking back over my life, I could not truly find the answer I was seeking. I've had good and bad things but to be happy, I could not say. The more I contemplated on the word the more I thought about it and no answer was found. Money was not the problem for now I am richer than my wildest dreams married to a woman I won't change for and have a woman on the side that wants to be my wife.

I forgot about Dandy my ghetto ass, snitching bitch that will tell on her own ass, if you listen to her. I don't have a clue as to what she is talking about, but I will call her and ask but not now. I have other things that are weighing on my mind that are of an importance. Frankly, I don't even know where I am with Solo. She may think that I don't love her enough but that is not it.

I desire to change but fuck. I will do it on my own time. Her telling me to change won't help me at all. It will only happen when I am prepared. I can't win from losing was the phrase that came to mind. It also makes me smile and truly miss OG Pete.

My grandfather always spoke some old wise saying and they were always on the money. Now I am thinking about him. I went from thinking about my wife to my deceased grandfather. I went from the living to the dead. Frowning, I felt sorrow and remote in a huge house that is fit for a queen.

What the hell am I doing? I am lying in bed thinking about a dead man and how his words still live beyond the grave. Turning over, I stared out the window and remembered when I was at Monica's house. It is there too that I stared out the window. I was in somewhere-somewhere land and didn't know if I would return, not even knowing what my thoughts were about. Turning to the other side, I closed my eyes for I needed to rest because I have a lot more work to do and staying awake is not going to help me.

I thought about Solo and how she was doing. The mention of her gave me chills for she has always been there for me and even if I hustled she knew that I loved her. We have been through so much and so much she deserves but to me that means to hustle harder. I never want her lacking or asking a motherfucker for anything. I am her husband, and my job is to provide for her. *That's what you do for the other women* my mind told me.

Yeah, I do try to provide for every woman that I ever had but with my wife it was funny how she never once complained about the money or the way I got it until now. I thought about the day she left. Truthfulness that entire week she had been off in her character even her attitude and performance was not the same. The more I tried talking to her the more she rebelled. It was like she was saying something, but I couldn't understand.

Mind you that I took classes on understand bitches but my own wife. I did not have a clue what she was yelling at me to get. Furthermore, the way she came at me about the recorded video message was just a ploy. When she left it drafted to change this, change that, do this or stop that. "Where did all the fucking nagging come from?"

I still with no idea and once she left she did not let me see her. I desired to see her, but it is she that wanted to leave. I let her ass go; nonetheless, it still did not and up. I replayed the conversation in my mind, I replayed it with my mouth, and I retracted the entirety of that day to make sure I did not overreact in any form. I tried to make sure that I did not overlook something and taking a pause, I concluded that I did not.

Why is my wife so persistent now that I change and be a diverse man than what she married? I can only accept facts if she did not love me. She clearly did not say so but her leaving me told me something different. We men don't communicate as we should, and this sounds like one of those moments.

After all the bullshit I do, I love Solo, but I cannot be the faithful man she calls for me to be. The streets are in me, and the hustle mentality stands firm and strong. I wish I could be someone different when I was younger but after having the knowledge, money and experience fuck being somebody else. I will be me, hands down. Taking a deep sigh, I went to bed with Solo on my mind so quite naturally I would dream about her.

CHAPTER 12

Solo and I were young. It was at this time that I did not care if she found out about what I was doing and who it is I was fucking. To put it frank, I did not care if she saw me with another woman, two for that matter. The worst part was I would go to her job at McDonalds and flaunt my new interest in her face. She even took our orders and watched me pretend to be all infatuated with the bitches.

The thing is she always came back to me. Irrespective of what I would do she came back to me. She could hear all types of shit on me and that did not bother her because she loved me. Solo could see me and not see me because she knows that if I am with someone else that's not the man she loves. The hurt in her eyes is something I vowed not to ever do, when we last departed. The last time she came back to me she said, "This is the final draw we bust up over pussy. I don't want to make this anymore habit forming than it is but if we bust up again it will be over dick. But think on this quote, "He that lives in a glass house shouldn't throw stones."

It took me damn near a month to understand what she meant. When I discovered that it means while you look at what someone else has and you think about destroying it, don't forget that you have a home that someone could destroy. I turned in my dream and opened my eyes. Sighing, I went turned onto my stomach and went to sleep. This time, I was almost eight. OG Pete and I were sitting on the back porch. One of his OG's came over and they walked off a few steps and talked. Then again, they may have been yelling because of their body postures. The guy walked off.

Given the impression OG Pete did not seem too pleased with his fellow worker. I only sat and watch as my grandfather came back to sit down. The other guy drove off in the car. OG Pete said, "He slick but he can stand another greasing."

Turning my head up towards my grandfather's words I in curiosity asked, "What does that mean, OG Pete?"

With a slight chuckle he stared at the other OG. My grandfather did not say a word right off. He appeared to be collecting his thoughts before he spoke to me but he later sparred, "It means that people think they are smart and they think they have gotten away with trickery, but they haven't. They think they can feed you bullshit, and you supposed to eat it up but don't. Many think they can lie and don't get caught but they eventually do. Basically, my boy, I'm saying just because you get away with it now doesn't mean you will get away with it later."

"Oh, why not say if you do wrong you will get in trouble? That is easier than the words you always speak."

"If it were easy all everybody would do it."

"I guess."
"Boy nothing in life is easy. If it is easy something is wrong with it."

"Is that just like saying if something is free something is wrong with it?"

"Boy you will always pay death and taxes and the only thing free is an ass whipping."

"How is that free?"

"The person that gave it to you didn't charge you for it."

We did a hearty chuckle about the free lesson. I looked up to my grandfather. I wanted to be an OG like him but better with more money of course. From the way he handled business affairs and from the countless women he has on his team, my grandfather was truly the kind of man that children wanted to be like.

As that encounter with OG Pete faded another one would come into play. This time the same OG I saw OG Pete talking to on many occasions was gathering sticks. From this angle, he looked to be making a fire in our backyard. He had two old worn tires, on the bottom, sticks and brushes on top, then another tire on top of that. Once he threw the gas on it, the blaze reached the sky.

I grabbed me a seat near the roasting fire because this was my first experience of country living. The OG gave me a bag of white cotton; which, I learned was marshmallows. He showed me how to put it on a stick and slowly twist it. When it was gooey, I put it between two graham crackers and tasted it. That snack was the weirdest but neatest snack ever. Before I knew it, I ate all but one; for it fell on the ground.

I picked up the stick and began burning the stick as I held it in my hands. This type of enjoyment was seldom indulged and highly foreseen. For I only heard about those things but never seen it for myself and growing up hustling, what the hell was a barn fire? Everything was great and there I saw OG Pete. He had on his favorite off gray suite with his matching hat and black Stacy Adam shoes. He was clean. He saw me playing in the fire with the stick. I would take turns burning the stick and then playing in the melted marshmallow. He came over to me and said, "Boy fire can make changes in your life."

"How so OG Pete?"

"Give me that stick."

I handed it to him, and he was playing in it like I was. I didn't see any change nor did I see a difference in what he was trying to tell me. Getting me another stick I began to play in the dark marshmallow alongside him. He didn't say a word as I continued to play. Without warning he put the burning marshmallow on the end of his stick and threw it at me. I reflex and it landed where I was sitting and not on me.

Genuinely the desire to ask him why he did that was upon me but no one questions OG Pete for shit, and I wasn't about to start. At that detailed moment he asked, "How you feel boy about the fire almost landing on you?"

"I didn't like it Sir. I was afraid for a moment."

"What you think you would have done if it landed on you?"

This is the time OG Pete needed to see that I was strong and can handle anything. With my chest poked out and base in my tone he replied, "I would take it like a man."

He moved his eyes to size me up and down. OG Pete finally stated, "A burnt child is scared of fire and if you play with fire you will get burned."

"What are you saying?"

"Meaning, you think you could handle it but when it comes back at you, it is then you will see."

"That makes sense."

I sat back down beside him and out of nowhere he stood up and tried to throw me in the fire. I woke up breathing hard and in a cold sweat. OG Pete's words were ringing louder than ever before. It was like a warning about something but from what? The more I laid there with my eyes opened I tried to figure it out but no luck. I know what the saying means but how is it being used towards me is beyond me.

After a few more moments of trying to figure it out, I came to me. As if realization hit me, I jolted up because I now know that it means; if you get hurt you will be skeptic about letting that hurt come to you again and if you play with something long enough it will eventually get you.

Who is the old saying warning from? What have I done? I tried to recollect my thoughts on who would want to hurt me? I am good to everyone, and I try to help people if I can; even the bitches that let me fuck them. It is not my fault if they fall for the shit I tell them. They are grown like I am grown and grown folks supposed to know shit when they smell it.

Closing my eyes again for sleep and it was not going to happen now. I swung me legs on the side of the bed and got up. I plan to remember this dream, so I sat there for a little while longer. I stood up and the first thing I saw out my window was my bench.   The bench redone is a keepsake because it is the only thing OG Pete has given me other than his sayings.

In truth, he is the only one that has watched over me and loved me. Mostly he is the reason why I couldn't leave the streets alone. As plain as day, I could see he and I sitting there looking at the few cars that came by. It was my birthday, and he wanted to talk to me alone. I was so sure that he has a surprise for me for he always did; although, lately my surprises were old folk sayings.

He use to tell me that words of wisdom will take me farther than any present could and no amount of dollars could take away the education of the brain. This was right before he went to jail, and it was the last time I saw him alive. My grandfather with his solemn face and weary eyes spoke with low demeanor, "You want to go camping, boy?"

Remembering that camping is something that only white people did, I was thrilled to do something that I only heard about doing so I screamed out, "Yes Sir!"

The look in his eyes told me that it was not the camping I was in search for. He gave me his famous smile and placed his arm around me to say, "Before you ever go camping boy, watch who you bring to the campfire because there are people standing around waiting to see you get burned."

I recalled the look on my face. Sure as we were sitting there. How could I have thought he would actually be giving me a surprise when lately his surprises are his words? Being who I am I asked, "OG Pete, why are you giving me these words and not gifts?"

He patted me head and said, "You play with gifts then you leave them alone, but words will stay with you even when I am gone."

"I don't understand this old folk saying."

"Before you go camping means before you set out to do what you need to do take inventory of what you want. Watch, who you bring to the campfire means after you have decided on who you want with you make sure they are with you. People standing around waiting to see you get burned means Jesus choose twelve men to follow him and out of those twelve, one still betrayed him. Boy in essence, no matter what you do there is someone always standing beside you waiting on you to fall."

I jumped up pissed and calling out, "What the hell has Mudcat done? That motherfucker!"

My pulse was racing like never before. This knowledge caused me to scramble to my feet and paced the floor. He is the only someone I could think of that is devious enough to try something. I love him but you have to keep his ass close to you and not out your sight. He comes back on the job for one day, and already I am getting negative vibes about his return.

Pieces of me hope that I am wrong, but I could not shake the ill sensation. No one knows my operation like he does, and no one is allowed around my wife but him. No one else knows about the bitches I had but him. He knows too damn much. My thoughts were spinning out of control as the spiraled downward fast as they came.

For the life of me, I could not think straight. Never before have so many sayings from my grandfather come close to me like they are now. The more I walked up and down my bedroom floor the more I couldn't think right. All the ideas I tried to avoid all turned to Mudcat. I could not think of anything to blame. Believe me, I tried.

No motherfucker wants to think that the motherfucker they took under their wing has betrayed them in some form. No man wants to take a fucker back that they know is like a hungry dog to steak. My head was beginning to ache for the very thought of Mudcat doing such a thing was phenomenal. With my hands on my each side of my temple, I continued to recall the old sayings, hoping I misunderstood but no luck.

My thoughts were running everywhere because I could not control them. I kept hearing those sayings over and over again. Back-to-back to back-to-back. It is to the point that I have tears in my eyes for being so angry over what I don't know. All I know is that my boy is close to me and somehow the warnings are about him.

Looking at the phone I desired to call him but didn't. One thing I have learned is that when you confront someone do it in person. They can hide behind a phone, but they can't hide their reactions in your face. Some reason or another, I needed to see his reactions. I began to stare outside, not knowing what to think. All I know is that OG Pete and his sayings have never steered me wrong and they have at all times been factual.

But this time I am refusing to accept what I think is true. I have practiced being patient, but this anger was flaring in me like none I know of. The more I thought about Mudcat's treachery the more upset I became. I tried calming myself down, but the rage was too far gone and too rapid to put out. Even though, I don't know the extinct of the disloyalty but from what I put together it would be off the charts.

In my heart, something was telling me that this is going to hurt me like never before. It is the way OG Pete's saying came at me. The way he spoke to me it was like you should have been listening to me and the things I told you. Regardless how I denied it, I cried even the more. The tears wouldn't stop and the more I tried to stop them the more they came. The urgency to call my wife was upon me but I could not call her for all the neglect I gave her would be held against me.

I knew she would understand but right now I needed to be alone with my thoughts. I have no earthly idea what this means, and I know if OG Pete is in my dream than it is a sign but for what, it's unknown. I looked-for someone to talk to and since I didn't want to call Solo, I called Monica. Sitting on the edge of the bed I waited for her to answer. The phone rang and rang. I knew that it was early in the morning, but I did not want to trust my own judgment. After a few rings, she picked up and spoke, "Are you alright?"

I was quiet as I calmed myself down to speak to her. Cautiously I said, "I dislike bothering you this early, but I knew you were awake. I need to talk to you."

"L. T. I was just reading, and you were on the brain and gland you called. I need to talk to you too."

"You go first" I told her,

"The time I spent making love, I mean fucking you was sensational, and it had opened my eyes to many things. I am forever indebted to you for how you made me believe in myself."

Flatly I spoke, "Are you not going to be my friend anymore?"

"Yes, but you must know that all because of you my ex-husband came to his senses. He realized how he has a great woman and how he let me go. We are trying to work things out and it has been great, thus far. We even go to church together and he has been more of a father to the children than he was while we were married."

"I am grateful to hear that."

"Thank you. It looks as if to me this rendezvous or escapade has worked out better for me. My husband no longer takes me for granted and he has pledged that he will spend the rest of his life making it up to the children."

"It's all about making the children happy, Monica."

"I know."

"If they aren't happy then as a parent your job is not finished."

"You know what?"

"What's that?"

"It's like the divorce and meeting you was the best thing that has happened to me. Our fling."

"Oh, that's what it was?"

Monica laughed and said, "I guess I found a name for it. Anyway, our fling made my distant husband a better man towards the children and me. He knows I met a man, and it hurt him like crazy that someone else had me, but he is not bitter. He told me that he realized that leaving his family was the worst mistake he had ever made. L. T. he is right."

"I hope all works out for you."
"You me! He has not moved back in of course and I am not quite ready for that but the children wants their daddy so it makes it harder for me."

"Do what you have to. I can't lie to you Monica the last time I was there, and your son said da-da. It did something to me. It was like I saw things from another prospective. I thank him for that and I thank you for allowing me to sample the pussy. I must add, it's damn good, it's a shame I didn't get a chance to taste it."

"You silly L. T."

We chuckled and she asked, "What is it that you needed to talk to me about?"

"Nothing."

"Nothing?"

"Yeah, nothing at all."

"So, you call me this early in the morning just for nothing?"

"Well, I got a chance to hear your voice and to know that you are doing well. That is great for you. I want you to be happy."

"L. T. I want you and your wife to be equally blessed. Maybe this separation will benefit you both like it did me and mine. We just don't know what the future holds we can only know when it comes to us."

"You right about not knowing because at one point you think you know then all of a sudden you are not sure anymore. As for my wife and I, it might but I can't say."

She yarned and I knew that she was sleepy. I said, "I am going to miss you and the children. Continue being a great mom to them and don't let another man let you feel that you are any less. Have a happy life."

"I will remember what you said and you both too, bye."

Silently I spoke, "Bye" but don't think she heard it.

I closed my cell phone and sat on the bed edge some more. Verbally I spoke, "It's good that someone is happy."

I was going to miss fucking her short fat ass but happy that she is doing what is best for the children. It has often amazes me how women are. A majority of them don't know their ass from a whole in the ground. On the other hand, some do. For those that have their priority in the right prospective, I like that. Monica is one of them. She is doing all she can for her children, and she makes them her top.

I don't think I could have her worshiping me and neglecting her children. Some men wouldn't care how a woman is to her children they only want her good to them. Feeling tired, I placed the phone on silent and with much on my mind I went in a deep sleep.

CHAPTER 13

I awoke feeling optimistic about my life. Whatever it is that Mudcat has done will not affect me this day. I'm going to call my wife and tell her that I want to do better if she will come home. I just pray it's not too late. I am going to go to church and do all that family shit she wants me to do. I just know that I can't go another night without her in my house, my arms and my life. I will spend every day making it up to her just like Monica's husband is doing for them.

Never did I realize that I had taken her for granted like I did when we were teenagers. I always got the notion that she would come back to me. Usually did but now I believe that this has altered my love for her on a higher level. If she comes back, I will not cheat on her I will be the most faithful man living and I will dedicate myself to her all over again.

I will not lose her, and I will forever be indebted to her for putting up with me and how I allowed the love of the streets to come between us. I am eager to hear her voice, and I am prepared to have her with me. It's funny how it took me dreaming about things my grandfather use to tell me to get me to see that I always had her love. It wasn't good enough for her to tell me for if she tells me, I don't hear that.

The spirit of pride had me convinced that I had it all planned to my way of liking. I would hear her, but my ears were numb because Solo never talked the things I desired to hear. Stepping into the shower no longer reminded me of Monica or the time we fucked in her shower. It was like it never happened. My mind was cleansed for all the things done wrong to hurt and offend my wife. I didn't think about Dandy or Lizzie, I only thought about Solo and how this time of year, her skin would glisten in the sun.

The way her hair hangs immaculately onto her silken honey, brown shoulders, it's enough to make a man go crazy. Then I must have been crazy to not have seen what has always been before me. How could I have let my wife leave me? If I wasn't stupid and only thought about money, Solo would be here with me now and we could have started on the family she desperately talked about. I've been ignorant to the fact that the streets never loved me they only take in. It is men like me that have thought only of themselves and not others.

The innumerable scores of women that I have run through didn't know anything about me. They only knew of the smooth talking gentleman that was at their every beck and call. They never knew that I was searching for what I have at home. How could Solo ever forgive me, when I have done her so wrong? I finished my shower with grace and changed clothes. I am optimistic and excited about the life my wife and I can have.

Money is not the option anymore because I have countless of dollars and we won't ever have to struggle. I even bought the house Solo always wanted with the spacious yard and picked white fence around the property. There is even a stable for a pony for our children one day. Picking up my cell phone, I saw that Mudcat called.

I listened to his message, and he said that he will be in later if not tomorrow because he is going to stop things with his ole girl. He also mentioned that he was grateful that I gave him another chance to work and get his self together. I was proud that he was doing better. Then I saw a miss call from Dandy. Something told me not to call her back, but she is still a renter on my property. As I dialed her number, I could hear *Misery loves company, misery loves company, and Misery loves company.* Before I could hear that saying again, Dandy said, "What yo ass doing this morning?"

"Huh, just stepped out the shower. Is everything alright at your place this morning because you are calling?"

"Yeah, but I need to talk to you on some real bitch shit."

"Ok, I'm listening."

"You know yo ass been knowing me for a long time and we had a history and shit."

"True."

"Damn Nigga cut a bitch short, why don't you."

"Dandy go on. I have some stuff to do this morning."

"Have you ever known me to be a liar or a home wrecker for that matter?"

That was an odd question for her to ask. Truth be told she is one of the most honest person I have met. It's true she is ghetto, ratchet and everything else wrapped up in between but to lie, that was not in her character. After thinking she interrupted me to say, "Damn yo ass have to think and shit if I am a liar or a home wrecker?"

"No, I was about to say that you may be ghetto acting among other things, but I have never known you to be a liar. You good people. You always let me know what's up by keeping your ears to the ground and your eyes to the sky. What is going on?"

"I first want you to know that it is never my intention to tell you anything that you don't need to know. I will lie fo yo ass, steal fo yo ass but this is some bullshit that I don't want to tell yo ass."

There was a pause because now my heart is sprinting in a race to know. Soon as she said never my intention a red flag went up and now my ears are attentive to her every word. I know that whatever the information is, it must be hard for her to tell me. Most of the time she comes on out and spills all she knows but this has to be something hard. Making up my mind to break the harsh silence I blurted out, "Are you going to tell me or what?"

"I am really debating if I should hang up now or what to be honest wit yo ass?"

"Dandy, you on the phone now."

"Let me ask, are you sure you want to know the information I found out?"

"Yeah, I am sure because you always keep me up to date on what is going on, why wouldn't I want to know?"

"Because this information is something that is not like any other facts, that I must tell yo ass."

"Go on and tell me."

"The word on the street is, yo wife is fucking up on yo cheating ass."

I guess her words didn't reach my brain because she said it again, "They told me that yo wife is cheating on yo ass."

"I don't think you got that word right."

"Shit yea the fuck I do. Hell, how yo ass think I felt when I heard it. Shit I asked again to make fucking sho they got the right person. They told me that she works as a secretary uptown, and she is married to Pete Times grandson. Shit, they ain't too many of yo last names around here and so I knew it is the right one. But to be more specific I asked them to describe her, and they say café' skin, shoulder length hair, firm face tender built, tiny waist with a small ass and questionable beautiful eyes."

A spirit of fury came over me like never before. My hands began to tremble and my nerves within me started quivering as if I were cold. I half trusted myself to speak. I needed to know what else is there for me to hear. Trying to sound calm I questioned, "Are you damn sure about this? Because if you are not, I'm going to get you and your informant for the damn mess you have caused."

"Hell yeah, I'm sure. You know I don't know what the fuck her ass looks like. I don't give a damn about what the fuck she doing, I give a damn about what the fuck yo ass doing. Hell, shit, why the fuck would I lie to you, huh? I knew that if you found out that I knew and I didn't tell yo ass then you will put time on my ass. Shit, I tell yo ass everything else I hear and knew this was not an exception."

"What damn word is that, to tell you that my Solo is fucking up on me? It better be the right damn word, Dandy!"

"Just the damn word on the street and that ain't all."

"No ghetto bitch you have to tell me something more than that."

"Hell yeah and shit now I don't want to tell yo ass a damn thang now."

"Yo ass better tell it!" I demanded of her.

"Fine don't hate me, I'm just the messenger."

"Dandy!"

"Yo cheating ass wife is fucking yo weak ass friend Mudcat."

Words could not describe the emotions that flooded me. I dropped my cell phone and stared at it. *Did she say Mudcat fucking my Solo? My Solo?* I in part did not want to pick up the phone and ask again because I hope she was wrong. One thing I know about Dandy is she makes sure it is accurate before she tells me and if she is telling me, then it is true. I can't believe it.

How the hell is this happening to me? I heard Dandy yell out, "Yo ass there!"

I picked up the phone and stated softly, "Yeah, I am here. How long they been fucking?"

"Do I really have to answer that question?" She said to prolong my answer.

"Yeah, yo ass needs to answer the question."

"They had been messing around about a week after she left yo ass. As for fucking about a month or so ago but I can't say if he ever hit it because no one knows for sure. It's only speculation."

"So, she was the woman he was talking about to me all this time?"

"From my understanding yes; he was telling you about yo own damn wife. My sources say he was pussy whipped."

When I heard that I placed the phone to my chest because my brain was not receiving that statement too well. I spoke, "Is she pregnant by Mudcat?"

"The word on the street is, she is pregnant, but they don't know if it is his or not because the timing is too close."

"Her ass pregnant?"
"Look I can only tell you what the word on the streets tell me and from this point she is pregnant but is concealing it from

everyone. If you don't pay any attention to her you won't be able to tell it. My source also says she has been wearing baggier clothes and shit."

I am stunned and outraged at the same time. How could she do this to me? How could she fuck and get caught by a motherfucker that will never love her or give her the finer things in life she deserves. Trying to disconnect myself from the information would not do me any good. I had to finish hearing what else is said on the streets about Mudcat and Solo.

"If it's any help his ass can't fuck like you, with his teeny tiny dick. I don't know what the hell she even can do with a small ass dick like that once she has had yo good dick ass. If I were you I would whip her cheating ass. I then would beat the brakes off his cutthroat ass. Ain't' no damn way I would grin in a motherfucker face and fuck his main thang. That's some killer shit right there if you ask me. Ain't no fucking way."

"Dandy do they know that I know?"

"Hell no! They ass don't know shit. What they didn't count on is the streets having eyes and ears everywhere. It's in the streets that you find out shit you normally wouldn't hear about. I love this life and not change it fo shit."

"Dandy I want to keep it from them that I know."

"L. T. if it is to any measure I want to say I know you a motherfucking dog but to have your closest dog work for you and then fuck yo wife, his dog ass deserves a damn beating if I ever did know one."

"Thanks for the heads up."

"Well, no matter what happens between us, you still my number one dick, even if yo ass don't ever get this ass again."

"Bye Dandy."

"Oh yeah my rent will be a little late."

"Ok, you good."

"Aight bye."

"Bye."

I felt like my world had caved in. Even as I sit here I still can't believe what I just heard. No matter how I play it, I still can't believe it. My wife and my boy fucking out of all the motherfuckers in the world she picked Mudcat. The further my brain lingered on the fact that he has touched my precious piece the more pissed off I got. The more I imagined his greasy ass busting a nut in her the newer my anger became.

When this fucker had nowhere to stay he stayed at my place. When he didn't have shit but the clothes on his back, I stepped in and put him on. When this low-down dirty motherfucker needed money to invest in his own place, I did that for him and when he needed to come back I took him back in. And the entire time he was getting the only pussy in town that I didn't share.

There were times when I put his drunk ass on pussy, and he still couldn't do shit. I was there for him. He knew that Solo, was a no dick zone. Still, he fell for my wife, my fucking wife!

That shit doesn't even sound good to say it in one sentence. My brain is still trying to grasp them together. I am now hearing impaired and incoherent. My thoughts are very unclear, and my heart is heavy and burden down.

For the first time in my life, I didn't know what to do. I shouldn't be angry but I am. Solo is not a bitch on the streets, she is my wife, and I don't share my shit at home. That low down dirty bastard is going to pay when I set eyes on him. Equally I want to hurt Solo so much, but I just can't. I can't come to terms to hurt her like I want to. I am in pain that she would even fuck but to fuck my boy, my right hand is too much to bear.

So many reactions are racing through me, and I don't know which one to choose from. I'm going to talk to her. I have too. I need to know everything I can but as for him he better pray to God that I have calmed down; for if I'm not it's his ass. Suddenly I recalled my dream. It was OG Pete, and he gave me the warning all about fire, but this fire I have now is like unto hell's fire and it's going to engulf Mudcat.

My thoughts began saying, *use me for a few moments to kill him and beat her. She is your wife and real women supposed to have some type of standard but where is hers? She fucked your home boy. Don't you hear how that sounds? She let the motherfucker you trained bury his nut deep into those pussy walls that you hunger after so much. He was probably laughing at you the whole time he was fucking her. Just think about it, she barely came by and he hardly worked. He more than likely gave her the ammo she needed to get out your way and fall for him.*

If you don't do anything now, you will be looked at as a weak pussy and other men will think they can be your friend and fuck what you have at home. You have to take a stand L.T. so this won't happen again. You have to set an example so others will know how to stay away from what is yours. You are Lamar Times and nobody makes a fool of the Times family. I know you remember those beatings you got because the family was shamed for you getting caught. This is one of those times.

Don't let bitch nigga like Mudcat get away for making you and your family look stupid. He even asked for his job back. He is going to take your money and take care of your wife. The last thing you need is to have a pussy name on the streets. Get that motherfucker and put that TIME on his ass. Teach him that what is yours is yours and what is yours is not to be fucking touched.

I started walking around to erase the thoughts that were attacking the peace I wanted to have but it did not help. I sat back down and rocked back and forth as I kept telling myself that it was a fabrication. The more I told myself that the more I tried to deny the pain and hurt that was all over me. However, I kept hearing, *L. T. you know how soft and ripe her skin feels and you know how her sweet and virtuous her pussy tastes. No man deserves the pleasure to have her goodness but you. No man needs to know how she squirms and smells up close but you. Close your eyes and see how she trembles when you are taking her.*

I closed my eyes as my thoughts told me, and I could see the way she moves under me and how innocent she appears when she is lost in my loving. I couldn't take it knowing that she has allowed a bitch nigga to sample what I delight myself in getting. I opened my eyes and heard, *Come on L.T. Solo is yours not his or anyone else for that matter. You know how she would suck you until you are exhausted with pleasure. Now she is doing that other nigga the same. She can't turn on or off the way she fucks or sucks in the bed. She is a woman so you know that a woman will put out the best just to reel a man into her loving arms. She is not going to short cut it because she is cheating and cheaters don't short cut when they making it good.*

You know how the game is played because you have played them on numerous occasions. You do recall her telling you that if you two break up that it will be about dick? Well, this is the dick she been talking about. That little dick bastard has been poking his little ass stick in your wife the one that was given to you. L. T. you can't let that shit ride. You are a damn man. You must stand up now and defend the Times family honor. OG Pete would be disgusted with you for not handling this.

I stood up as if I were possessed. My thoughts were right. If by chance this is the devil that Solo talked about is feeding me the thoughts I desperately lingered on, then so be it. The hours chipped away as I walked around in my room practicing how to act calm and unsuspicious. That task alone was proving to be a challenge. On the other hand, I was finalizing it better than I thought. For some reason I have the design on how I would carry out this strategy. My test finally came Solo called.

"Hey babe, how you doing?" I asked her sweetly.
"I am feeling better."

"What's been wrong with you?"

"I been having this bug that I need to address with you. When will you be free to talk?"

"I'm available all afternoon. Mudcat is not here today so today will be perfect, if you don't have any plans."

"No today is perfect. I will come by soon as I leave up here."

"Ok babe I look forward to seeing you and when you come pull up in the back. I am having work done on the front entrance."

"Ok. Will do, bye."

"Bye, love you."

"Love you too."

Soon as I hung up with her, I felt a spice of wrath towards her. Just hearing her voice sounding so guiltless and sweet caused my skin crawl. By that it almost gave away my true intentions.   I went out the door to the shop when the next thing I know, Mudcat was calling. I didn't want to answer the phone, but I knew that I must. Gradually I slurred out, "Hey Nigga what's up wit ya?"

"Nothing, you at the shop?"
"I'm walking across the yard to the shop as we speak."

He paused and when he did that, I knew that he had something to say. To encourage him I spoke, "Yeah, I'm at the shop. What's on your mind?"

"I need to come in later on today to talk to you about that woman friend of mine."

I plan to talk to Solo for about an hour, so I said to my unsuspected friend, "Be here in less than two hours. I have a prior engagement to attend. When you come up pull in the front, I am doing something to the back driveway. "

"Ok. Let me tidy up some shit here then I will be on my way."

"Ok, see you in a few" I spoke with ease.

"Later."

"Later."

The phone conversation ended as I unlocked the door of the shop. Turning on the air, I went into my office and closed the blind to the inside office window. I proceeded on to sit in my office chair because I now know how to strategically make a careful move. Placing my legs on the desk, I crossed my feet and put my hands while my thumbs rested under my chin, to think.

The longer I sat there no good ideas came to my mind. I could only think of killing him and watching him die in his own piss and blood. I twisted my head from side to side as if I was trying to shake off the perverted ideas that still remained in me.

Jumping upright I know how he is to pay for his disloyalty. Like a mad scientist on a mission to create his final creation, I began to work with speed before Solo arrived. I was moving this and that around by thinking "What if I were him and how would I get away" therefore, I put tools and etc. in the path to slow down the getaway. With one final look, everything looked normal. I then placed my seat so I could see Mudcat when he came.

A short while later Solo pulled up and she parked around back just like I asked. I know that if Mudcat came and saw her car he would not stop. I must make sure her car was unseen and place her in a position to be helpless. With evil intentions, I smiled at her as she came through the back door. Locking the door behind me, I hid the malicious thinking on my face. She never noticed it.

This is the first time I am redefining my love and observing the woman that I loved for many years. Her hair has grown and her skin glowed, she even has a slight weight gain. *She's definitely pregnant* I heard my thoughts tell me. Giving her my usual cheerful smile, I gave her a light kiss and spoke, "You look lovelier than ever, Solo. You almost look like you are glowing."

"Thank you and trust me I don't like I'm glowing."

"Come on, walk this way."

Solo walked in front of me to our office. Checking my watch, I had about an hour before Mudcat was to arrive; therefore, I put things into motion. She went in the office and sat down. I came in behind her and sat across from her as I asked, "How are you my love?"

With the smile she has given me for years, she somehow still touched my heart. Even though I am angry, I still love the shit out of her. In actual fact, what I am experiencing is to some degree what I think she would be going through, but she is not. I am.

"I am great, and you look wonderful, L. T."

We come within reach of the office door, and I scooted in front and opened it for her; like always. She walked by and smiled. That perfume she always wore hit my nostrils and it makes this moment harder to comprehend. I closed the door. She took a seat in the chair across from my desk. I in return, sat in my chair and we only smiled.

"Oh yeah, thanks for telling me that I look wonderful, sorry I was slow to respond. I guess it's the lonely nights I've spent without you by my side; with only wishes to hold me and faith to keep me."

"Awe. You have always been a romantic."
"Only when it comes to you, my dear."

"I know yup I know."

"So, tell me wife, what do I owe the pleasure to have you come by my office on today?"

"I can't come see my husband?" She spoke in a positive manner.

If I was blind to her, I would have bought her tone, but I am on to her and can't wait to expose her for the cheater she is. Yet I was just as pleasant to her to say in a mellow tone, "You are always welcomed to see me. You just didn't come to see me. I didn't want you to think that I was pressuring you, so I decided to wait until you came to me or told me to come by."

"You were right, in partial. I didn't want you to come see me. I had my reasons."

"Reasons? Reasons like what that you should have about seeing me, your husband?"

"Let me start from the beginning so you can kind of understand my reasons."

"That is a great place to start because I really want to know all about it."

She humored me with a slight laugh and shook her wonderful strands of hair. That used to get to me but now that didn't do shit for me. I spoke with humor back at her, "I'm waiting, sometime today, Solo."

"You and I have been through so much."

I cut her off and spoke, "Save the warm up announcement. Start at where we are at now. You don't have to remind me how hard I hustle."

Solo must have sensed the tension as she said, "You are angry about something? I can come back and talk later."

"Maybe I am but it has nothing to do with you. Plus, if you say you will come back you may not. Do you know how long it has been to get you here?"

"It has been a minute."

"Right so go on, you have my full attention."

"Seriously?"

"The thing I am angry about will not affect me listening to you."

"How you going to listen to me with clarity if something else is bothering your mind?"

"You know I can multi-task."

"Ok, to begin with, I know you have other women even if I can't prove it or see it with my own eyes."

"Seeing it with your own eyes is the best way that way you know it is true, but you left. So, continue because that is water under the bridge."

"I received a video message with only a man's voice; which, is supposed to be yours but that is not why I left."

"This sounds interesting."

"I left because I found out something. I didn't know how to tell you and to be honest me telling you what I discovered would had you more money hungry than ever. So, I used the high road by saying, I want you to find your way to do right."

"What you mean do right? Shit you aren't starving or lacking for anything. I have always done right by you. You may not agree but you never had to worry about any woman, man boy or beast coming at you about any bullshit."

Raising her tone up a notch she said, "Wrong! I left because I was in lack of my husband."

We continued to glare at each other without words being said. I felt the hurt, and I know she felt the hurt as we held our pose for a few more moments longer. With a more lax tone my wife continued, "I was in lack of my husband. You provided money for us no doubt. You always had a way for us to have what we need but I needed companionship. I needed to be your support, not be supported. That is one reason why I got a job. I thought if I worked you could notice my contribution, and we could have meaningful conversations, but you only buried yourself deeper into your shop and clients."

Sitting up in my seat, I spoke, "Like hell you were in lack of your husband. I was still making love to you, and I was there any time you needed me. I would ask how your day was and even rub your feet when I was there but most of the time, I was gone at night meeting clients and making business deals for us to have better."

"What better is a seventy thousand five hundred square foot home with no one to share it with? What good is going on luxury vacations alone? Huh? What good is it?"

"It's every bit of good when you can do it. Not many women I know of can say the same. They would be honored to have a chance to do half the things you have done and then some. All you do is complain and want me to stop my way of doing things."

"You were still making love but to who? You did all those things you spoke of but I didn't mean physical. I needed a husband to be faithful to me and only me. I deserved to be happy. We can be having sex and if you get a client call, you stop pleasing me to go to them."

"Damn Solo, they talking about ten to fifteen thousand dollars. Damn right I'm after that paper."

"You have left me unpleased too many times and yet I stay faithful. You know why I stay faithful?"

"Why?"

"Because I love you, even when I did not feel your love, I believed you loved you. I didn't go by what it looked like I went by what it was. There have been times when I needed to just hear your voice, but I never got that. Some days I felt like low and all I needed was to hear from you or for you to take me into your arms and tell it's going to be ok, but you never once did that. Sometimes I would try you by not speaking to you but you only ignored me and stayed gone. I ran out of options. "

"Why did you not come out and tell me?"

Raising her tone up a pitch she concluded, "Why should I? When you knew me like the back of your hand. You know everything about me and with you I don't know you at all. All this money changed you and it desensitized you. You got to the point, that you were more in tuned with the streets than with me. You acted like you could not see how the streets were ripping at this marriage. To me you didn't care anymore. You became a L. T. that I no longer realized or thought highly of."

"How long have you claimed to be feeling this way?"

"For a very long time and when you are schedule to do things with me, you take a reign check and send Mudcat. You were sending another man to be the man for you."

The mention of his name on her lips did something to me. I sat back in my seat and tilted my eyes to the ceiling just so I did not show my true identity of the matter. Regaining self-control I said, "Yes, I sent him because I trust him and there would be no other man that I would have near you, than him."

"L. T. you never wanted to spend time with me or just be with me."

"Solo. Are you fucking serious?"

"Yes."

"Every damn thing I do was for you. I hustled for you. I buy, sold and traded for you. I have devoted my life to the streets so you can have the finer things in life. You don't have to work you chose too. You don't have to do a damn thing but shop every day if you wanted."

"And I appreciate it but those things did not make me happy. It made you happy. Money did not claim me, it claimed you. I could have lived on a poor man's salary as long as I had you. It didn't matter about the richer things."

"It matter to me because I never wanted to see a wife of mine working or going without material things and me for that much. I never planned for my wife to do anything she didn't want to do."

"You are missing the big picture."

"What is the big picture?"

"You have neglected me. You never spent any of your hustling street time with me. Every waking moment you devoted it to the world. They would call you and you came running. I would call you and you would send Mudcat."

Very bluntly I said, "We have already had this conversation before. Get to the point that is what I want to hear."

"Endlessly I tried communicating with you, but you never heard me. Many days I would come to your shop to talk but you were always busy so I would leave. Have you not noticed how withdrawn I become to you?"

"No, I just thought you were on your monthly or something."

"You know women just like I know men. All the signs were there, you just did not want to see them."

"What the fuck you mean? I always paid attention to you."
"Fixing your food and fucking me does not constitute paying attention to me. I always had to wait my turn just to talk to you. L. T. I felt unimportant in your life, and I just could not have that, so I left with regards that you would get it together."

"You mean you left on a damn voice message recording."

"Yes, someone you know sent it and being that I could not prove it was you, I let that slide."

"What gives for today? Tell me that. What makes today so fucking special that you came in to tell me all this bullshit?"

"I am getting to that."

She placed her hand on her stomach, and I pretended not to notice it nor was I going to ask her if she was ok. The feeling of uncaring is upon me and I don't think it wants to go away.

"As you were saying?"

"I remove myself from your life with a greater agenda. I needed to get out your way so you can find me essential to you. Regretfully I think it only made you worse off. I expected you to come after me but you only pretended that I was off on some extravagant vacation."

"Is that what you thought?"

"Yes, I did think that. If I was not here I needed you to miss me and stop your behind the doors job and work like average men."

"I missed you the moment you drove off, but do you know how hard that is in today's time to live the way we do? You have no idea how hard it is to stay number one?"

CHAPTER 14

Solo looked at me as if I was talking in another language. Then she said, "I think I better get to the point before I lose my nerve and leave here the same way I came."

The phone rang, and she gave me an evil eye. I picked up the phone and said, "Hello."

"Times I have four SUV's coming your way the later part of next week."

"Ok I will call you back later. I am in the middle of something."

"Ok."

"Some things never change."

"They do but I'm waiting on you to tell me but you talking about everything but why you have come. You have known me for almost all your life. Just come out and tell me and stop all this fishing for the right ass words to tell me."

"May I do this my way?"

Taking a pause, I spoke without moving my mouth. I nodded, "Yes my darling wife you may have it your way."

"When you showed no interest in changing, I started talking to someone and I know the word on the street has gotten back to you that I do know. But the word on the streets doesn't really know. The streets think they know but they only go by what they hear. They are on the outside looking in."

I sat up because she is almost opening admitting to me that she is or has been seeing someone. Not to give it away, I sat back in the chair as to rest while I wait on her to talk more.

"Before you and I go on you should know, I love you and now is the time for you to believe me. Believe that I would do anything to make our love the best love it can be in Christ."

"Right now, and how you feel about me or us has nothing to do with you talking someone or really talking to someone."

"I am seeing someone, but it is not the way you think and it's definitely not the way the streets portray it. But he is someone you know he is like a mutual friend."

"I know too many people and I didn't know that you fooled with too many people."

Taking her time, she acted scared as her voice quivered, "He is someone that is dear to me but like family to you."

Solo began to swallow hard. I had tears in my eyes and I spoke softly as if I didn't believe the words, I was about to speak out loud, "Mudcat. Are you seeing Mudcat?"

She did not say anything. I said, "You sure it is the same Mudcat that works here with me and the same Mudcat that I took in under my wing and made my right hand man?"

I activated my voice higher as I shouted out, "The same Mudcat that I would have done anything to help? The one person in the world; which I would trust alone with you? Please tell me, he is not the same one?"

As if she didn't understand the questions I was asking, she spoke at to patronize me, "L.T. please it is not what you think. He is the same one that has always been there for you but let me finish explaining."

Speaking in a hard audible tone, I commanded before getting outraged, "Please tell me before I jump to conclusions."

My wife began to cry. Now this is a new one. She never cries easily. She did say she was pregnant and from what I hear pregnant women are emotional. Like usual, Solo blotted in to scatter my thoughts, "It's not just that. I'm pregnant."

Soon as those words hit my brain from my ears, I yelled out with surprise, "You what! Yo ass is what?"

"Can you please sit down and listen to me first before you get angry?"

I didn't know that I got up out my chair. Once I realized that I was standing, I knew I must remain seated. The last thing I am trying to do is make her fearful. I need her here for a reason and if I am upset she would try to leave. Calming down, I placed my bottom back into the seat and silently, asked, "Are you or are you not pregnant?"

"Yes, but wait."

"What is there to wait on? You just dropped two explosives on me at once and all you can say is but wait. What the hell do you expect from me woman? A man doesn't hear every day that is wife is fucking his best and she is pregnant."

"I didn't exclusively say I was fucking him, I said I was seeing him there is a difference."

My love, my wife was sitting in front of me telling me she was pregnant and not just pregnant but fucking my best friend exclusively or not, what the hell ever. I continued to sit there not trusting what I would do to her if I got up. At this moment I am almost speechless and unfeeling. She cut off my thoughts as she trembled, "I'm pregnant and that was the other reason why I stayed away. I needed you to change for the best, but it did not happen. When I realized it was not happening, I decided to keep my distance. I prayed and I prayed on what to do but it was coming at a slower pace. You got to believe me. I had no idea that I was pregnant when I left."

"No idea huh?"

"I had no idea that I was pregnant and when I found out, my reasons changed."

"How the hell should it affect me? You did not tell me but how long had Mudcat known?"

"I told him a few days ago."

"So, you are the woman he was seeing that made him change to be a better man?"

She did not say anything. She only sat there with her head down. I hurled out more words to her, "So you the one that was going to help him do his bookkeeping work?"

"Yes."

"You don't work at the Courthouse."

"Yes, I do. I changed a few weeks ago because I could make more money."

"You mean you changed careers and did not tell me?"

"Why would I tell you and we aren't together. You were busy and I assumed that I could make my own decisions without you. I am grown and if you had called me enough you would have known."

"If your ass would have contacted me more you would have told me. How long does it take to pick up your damn cell phone; which, you have to your ear all day anyway just to tell me that you have changed jobs?"

"That is not the point."

"What the hell you mean that is not the point? You're seeing another man, pregnant, changed careers and not coming back to me because I have not changed to your liking. How and the hell can you say that is not the point to me!"

"I assumed that you were busy as always."

"Fuck the bullshit. Let's get back to this damn baby growing in your fucking belly!"

"What does it matter? You won't listen so I'm done discussing the baby!"

I stood up and came at her. Solo possessed a nervous glee in her eyes as I towered over her faster than she could get up. Snatching her up with one arm, I twirled her back to the window as she placed both shaking arms onto mine. I stared into her eyes and all I could hear was *hit that bitch in her face. Her lying ass knew what the hell she was doing. Her ass was just playing you until the streets told you of her bullshit. Fuck her and that baby she carrying. She deliberately fucked him, and she purposely tried to make you look stupid. Just look at her. Look at the way she stares? She doesn't think she has done anything wrong.*

Before I could give into the conscious of my mind we heard the sound of brakes scrubbing. I saw it was Mudcat. I smiled and let her go. She staggered backwards a few feet then she walked around me towards her seat. I went over to the window and closed the blinds so she could not see Mudcat's car and warn him in some form. I'm going to hear his side because I know bitches lie in distress. Changing my facial expression and to be sounding so believable as if I were up for a Tony Award, I spoke, "I am so sorry I snatched you. I don't know what came over me. Solo, you do know that I have never shown this much anger before. You forgive me?"

"Yes, I do but get rid of whoever it is so we can finish talking. You are going to be amazed through it all."

"Ok. I will be right back. Make yourself comfortable as I go check this out."

"Before you go."

She then asked, "What are you going to do?"

"Nothing. You have told me everything. What can I do? I may have lost my wife and my heart in one visitation."

"Mudcat is innocent in all this and once you hear me out you will finally know why all the secrecy."

"I know he is, but someone just pulled up. You stay in here while I let them know that I am closed for the rest of the day. Go on and have a seat."

Solo sat down. I closed the door behind me as I walked out. I went over to the car that Mudcat was working and began stooping down like I didn't know what I was doing. I had to break the lug nuts down before I could jack the car up. A few seconds later he came in. The closer he came the more I could feel the fuel igniting. If I ever needed to put on a show, now was the time. Swallowing like never before, I said, "Good you came. I was about to take off this tire but shit my back aches."

He extended his hand to me. Probably the same one he used to touch my wife. I placed the tire tool in his hand nicely as he spoke with cheer, "You know yo ass hasn't' done manual work like this in years. Let me help you. If I don't, you will be here all damn day trying to change a tire."

I moved out the way and allowed him to unloose the bolts. With his back to the office door and me between him and Solo I said the statement with fun, "Shit, you right. I only paint and do paperwork. The dirty work is for niggas like you."

We laughed as he stooped down to jack up the car from the side. Doing my best to get him to talk, I asked with concern "What's been going on? You sounded like you have a lot of shit on your mind."

"Man, I do. It's just that I fell and I fucked up."

"We all do that shit because pussy is a thing that men love to get and that soft wet shit will make any man do shit they normally wouldn't do."

"You right but I fucked up big time."

"How the hell you fuck up?"

"It started out as a helping a friend, but I wanted to take it to another level."

"The pussy must have been good as hell for you to want to claim the pussy."

"Shit it's not about the pussy it's the person that owns the pussy."

"Well how did that work out?"

"Shit it didn't. I fucked up. I should have waited."

"You a hard-working man and women should love to have you on their team."

"Yeah, but my ass is not caking like yo ass is."

"Little nigga you have to manage your finances and put a limit on the things you are willing to buy and get. Now buying pussy is something I don't do."

He chuckled at that thought because we both know he will buy some ass in a minute. Deciding To change his thought process into overdrive and plunge in on his weakness, I spoke with a hint of enthusiasm, "You know I have realized that I have taken my wife for granted and should have been there for her."

"Shit happens."

"Hell yeah, I have had my share of pussy to last us both a lifetime and then some but it has always been Solo that I cannot leave alone."

"She yo wife, you not supposed to leave her alone."

"True but those other hoe's gone bye-bye."

"Even the one with the kids?"

"Yup. I talked to her last night, and we agreed to be just friends and that's it."

"Hell, you done tapped the ass fuck being the friends. You know once you fuck'em friends are the last thing that comes to play because bitches get attached with the dick then they do underhanded shit to break up yo home; especially if you don't want them like that anymore."

"Damn yo ass has been taking notes, huh?"

"Hell yeah because that is almost how I got fucked up."

"How so?"

"I fell for her, and she wasn't feeling me the way I assumed but it's all good."

I decided to tell him about Solo, so I concluded, "I talked to Solo today."

"You did?"

"Yeah, and we are not on the same page as for her coming home."

"Isn't that the reason why she left so she can come back and y'all work out the kinks or something like that?"

"Supposed to be but some shit happened while she was gone. I guess I played too long or I just wasn't the right player."

"You mean you not the right player?"

"Hell no she is not coming home."

"Then what the hell y'all been doing?"

"I guess killing time."

"Did she at least tell yo ass why?"

"She told me that she has found a love in someone, and he has been there for her than I could. She said all kinds of shit."

"Shit like what?"

"Shit about a nigga that I knew of."

He stopped taking what he was doing and spoke, "Really? I mean she really told you some shit?"

"Yeah, and I was hurt but look at all the shit I have done to her. She can't help but find another to take my place."

"Yeah, nigga you have done a lot of shit to her."

"She even told me she forgave me and I told her that I forgave her. She went on to say that she cared a lot about him and she knows he loves her beyond the moon."

"I was going to tell her that I was giving up all this illegal activity of the business just for her. I was about to tell her that I will leave the streets alone for her, but I couldn't."

"Why?"

"What was the point? She stood up and told me to my face of her love for another man. That is something too many people don't do to me. I applauded her for her strength and determination."

"You can't help but love her. Your wife is different from anyone I have seen before."

"I know but I told her that she can divorce me and go be with him."

"What? How did that go?"

"It's ok but the worst part is she told me she was pregnant by him."

"Are you serious? She really told you she is pregnant?"

He dropped the tire arm and began unloosing the lug bolts slower. I then said, "She told me she was seeing someone, and she don't want to be with me because I have not changed."

"She did?"

"Yeah, and it hurt likes hell. Especially all the shit I have done to make sure he is not lacking for shit."

"Hell yeah I feel ya on that."

"Yo ass doesn't quite feel me on that."

"What do you mean?" He said as he laid the rest of the bolts on the ground.

"She told me her ass is seeing yo ass."

"Oh hell no, L. T."

He started denying it but I added, "But it's cool."

"It is?"

"Yes, because I know she has found someone that I know and yo ass is a hard ass worker. As long as you keep working for me, I'm good."

"Damn you mean that?"

"Why the fuck would I not? We boys and have been boys long before I met her. Shit I love her and that shit you can't change but hell with all the pussy I can get, why not let you have the one you never thought you could get."

"You alright L. T. I never thought you would be so cool about me being in love with Solo but damn you know when a better man has come along. She won't believe it when I tell her."

He didn't see it coming. The tire tool in my hands and I was playing baseball on that damn nigga's head. Blood splattered all over my face, neck and into my eyes. He was hollering as he fell up against the car. I didn't give a shit. I was hitting that backstabbing bastard all over his back, legs but mostly that head. Everywhere I saw an opening on him I was swinging.

"L. T. NO!"

I stopped swinging and to hear Solo's alarming voice. Given the impression she was stunned as her vision took in me with a dangerous weapon in my hands. I looked at her and spoke harshly, "GET YO ASS BACK OR I'M COMING YOUR CHEATING ASS TOO!"

Solo backed up and ran into the office. I became unease about her running into the office. Then it hit me, I forgot to unplug the damn office phone. I know she is calling the police because she is scared. I then took off towards the door, but it was lock. Trying to be calm I spoke, "Honey, open the door."

She was mumbling something. I looked through the inside office window, but the lights were turned off. With an outline of her body, I saw her curled up in the corner not far from my desk with the office phone to her face. I knew that the glass was bullet proof so I then I got stern in my speech to her, "Solo hang the damn phone up now!"

Solo with fear all over her glanced my way and began crying louder. Realizing that she is probably traumatized I raced to the door and each time I hit on the door, I said to her "Get off that damn phone! Solo open up! I'm not going to hurt you. I love you."

She still did not come to the door. I became angry as I screamed out at her, "Hang up now before I break this door down and get your cheating ass!"

"Open this fucking door, NOW SOLO before I break this bitch in!"

She would not open it. I then began banging harder on the door. I was trying to rip the door off its hinges, and it was not working. From behind the door, Solo kept screaming and crying like never before. Some of me wanted to stop but something in me would not let me. It was like there was no choice but to get her.

I stopped banging and I heard her stop crying. Suddenly I threw my body into the door to open it and she started back. I heard Mudcat moan, so I went over to him and began kicking his bloody body like a damn player on a soccer team. From behind me I heard, "THIS IS THE POLICE. PUT YOUR HANDS UP OR I WILL SHOOT!"

I wanted to stop but something in me would not let me. I felt driven to continue with my attack as I continued and then he warned me again, "STOP OR I WILL SHOOT."

At that moment, I stopped. He then said, "Raise your hands to the sky and walk back towards the sound of my voice."

I stood over Mudcat as he was bleeding and banged up body laid helplessly on the floor. I knew then he would never touch shit else of mine again. I then began to obey the police. Taking my time, I lifted my hands and walked backwards ever so slow. Once I got close enough, he spoke, "Now get on your knees."

I was beginning to get on my knees when I saw another officer come out of my office with Solo under his arms. She was hysterical and hyperventilating. Seconds later they were out of my sight. Once I got on my knees, he spoke, "Now lie down on your face and place your hands behind your back, nice and slow."

I did as he asked and he and a few more men came and handcuffed me. When they picked me up, I could nothing but blue uniforms and red and blue lights flashing. Soon as they got me out, the EMT's came in and went towards Mudcat's bloody body. The arresting officer then began repeating my rights; which, I hadn't heard in years.

Solo was in another police car across from me. She looked at me with displeasure on her face and a question in her heart. They placed me in the car and then they rushed Mudcat's body out to the ambulance. I felt some grief for him because he fell weak to pussy. As the police officer drove off with me in the back, realization kicked in. My ass is going to jail over some pussy but not just any pussy but my wife's pussy. I really can't believe that I may have seriously injured or killed my best friend because he fell in love with my wife and impregnated her.

The closer we got to the police station I could only see Solo's face as she cried with hurt. I have never wanted to see her cry or even look at me the way she did, but she did. I sat back and closed my eyes because I was blinded at the fact my wife always says don't let the devil use you and I did. I fell for him talking me into doing serious crime. God only knows what I would have done if I had broken into the office where she was. I may have killed her and or her baby. I don't know what I would have done if I physically harmed her.

We arrived at the station, and he opened the door. The cop said before taking me in, "I have always respected The Times family because my grandfather used to be a part of the organization. OG Pete took my grandfather in and kept him off the streets. All because of that I wanted to grow up protecting the streets on the legal side."

"Man."

He cut me off to say, "Don't say anything that can be used against you."

"I wasn't."

The white officer walked me in ahead of him with his hand on my arm. He led me into the processing room as they took all kinds of pictures of me being covered in blood. Once they did that I had to strip. They took my clothes and placed them in a bag; I assume for forensic. I washed off and put on their blue jumper and white shirt. They took my fingerprints and mug shots without the blood.

"You will have to go before a judge on Monday because it is the weekend."

"That is fine."

Time did not pass by as quickly as another officer placed me in my cell alone. All was crazy for me as those doors slammed shut. It's just me and my mind in this small cell. I remained standing and gawking at the back of the back wall. This is surreal as I imagined something out of the ordinary. I stood a few hours longer until my feet felt numb.

I have no idea what I was waiting for as I stayed in the same spot. I recalled occasions when OG Pete's OG would come and get me when I messed up and got in trouble. However, they all are long gone, and I must get myself out of this dilemma. I finally took a seat on the concrete looking built in bench. It was half the width of my body so I understood instantly that my side would be the only way. I then stretched out and glared at the side wall with nothing particular on my mind.

Solo did not come to my thoughts and Mudcat did not come to my thoughts. I thought about her child and how if I have to go sit down for years for fucking up my work partner, then I will do that. I will make sure her child does not suffer for what I did. That too does not matter that I am not the child's father. The more I thought of that, the more I lay on my side and glared. The night before court, I thought I saw OG Pete as plain as the wall I was looking at.

My grandfather wore his pin striped gray suit with the brim to match. That was the exact same suit he was buried in. I pinched myself and I did not wake up and nor did I holler. I sat up and stared at the vision before me. This time he said, "Many years ago I told you to get out the game and you didn't listen. You changed your game up but that was all you did."

I did not say a word for I felt like I was dreaming of him. I could not speak nor did I want to. OG Pete was here in person and not just speaking to me like his sayings usually does. He then said, "Boy, you have a tough breast in your mouth, but somebody has to suck it."

I still did not say a word because I was not getting this saying. He must have noticed my lack of understanding for he then said, "You make your bed hard you have to lie in it."

Now that saying I understood for it was very familiar to me. Before I could muster up words, he began to walk off into the wall. He then stopped and faced me again and asked me a question, "Those streets were here before you were born, and they will be here when you die. Did you find what you was looking for in those streets?"

Just like that he was gone, and the cell was dark again. This time I stood up and stretched for the cement was hard and very unpleasant. I then began to pace the small area. I summon up all the talking my wife and I did before she left. She used to tell me that I don't understand how easy it is for the devil to use us. Solo even went on to say that although I was not doing physical damage, I was doing damage. Who would have thought that having a chop shop was bad? I didn't. Now I am in jail because I listen to my conscious; whom, she also says is the enemy when we do bad things.

The entire time I thought about how I listened to that horrible voice hyping me up to hurt Mudcat and how evil I was to think of hurting my love. I made a poor choice and now look at me. I'm in trouble and my best friend could die. Then what have I accomplished? What could I do to rewrite the wrong that I showed to him and to her for this difficulty? I found myself in the same category as doing the very thing women do to other women by fighting over dick, and permitting dick to make them do stupid ass shit.

Those streets fucked me and the entire time I thought I was doing the fucking, but I wasn't. The God of this world, the devil and his imps sent me up a creek without a paddle and now here I am, fucked up and broken up over pussy. All weekend I sat here and think about my actions. It was the nighttime that bothered me. I could not get my wife's intense facial expression as she saw me swinging away on Mudcat.

I felt like crying because of the shit I allowed to cross my mind and most of for the shit that listened too. In my dream, I was crying and I heard Solo say her favorite word, "Pray."

I opened my eyes, fell on my knees to for humbleness and spoke, "Lord I don't know how to pray as I should, but I know you know the heart. I am a sinner, and I am not worthy of your grace. Please look down on me and have mercy. I confess today the known and unknown sins. I am that unworthy sinner, but you are my one and only Lord and Savior. I know that if any man comes to you any other way he is a thief. I am he, that thief, that sinner, that liar, that whoremonger, that backstabber, that cheater, I am he. I am asking you to change my ways and cleave me from all unrighteousness. I can't change my past but with you I can change my future. I ask this day that you continue to love me and keep me; in spite of me. However, situations plays out in my life I still know you love me. In Jesus name Amen."

Monday morning came and still no sign of Solo. But this day I am at peace. Whatever the judge tells me I am fine with it because I am now saved. When it comes to my wife, I know she has things on her mind, and I know she is very angry. None of that matters. I need to feel that she is still with me. I messed up band and I need her to forgive me. These streets have invaded me and my home for the last time.

My lawyer came by and stated that Mudcat was in a coma and because he was allegedly going with my wife I may get off. My lawyer left out and the police came in to shackle me before I am to enter the court room. I still did not see my wife. They took me to the front as I sat among other criminals. When the judge came in, we all had to rise and once he was seated, we were seated.

Still no sign of my wife but I did not let that bother me. Finally, he called my name. The officer escorted me to my seat. I could not sit. I stood by my lawyer.

"Mr. Times, you are charged with aggravated assault, how do you plead?"

"I plead guilty."

"Is there anything you want to say?"

"Your Honor, I've already asked Christ to have mercy on me and it's in his hands."

"Very well, come back tomorrow for sentencing."

The police came over to me and took me back to my cell. My lawyer said, "You are going to beat this, and my sources tell me that he is in ICU and is expected to have delays, but he will not die."

"That is so good to hear."

I went back to my cell and then the officer came and said I have a visitor. They handcuffed me and took me to the two-way mirror. When I got there, it was Solo. My smile grew like never before. It felt wonderful to see her and she looked beautiful. She sat down and picked up the phone. I waited until she was seated before sitting down to answer the phone.

"Hello."

"Hi."

"How are you and your baby?"

"You mean how am I and our baby are?"

When said that I quenched my eyes and said, "Huh?"

"Mudcat was just a friend but he did fall for me and showered me but I did not love him. He knew that but I offered to help him do the paperwork for his business, but he wasn't making enough money to stay afloat. He confessed to wanting to break us up but was too afraid to do otherwise. I told him that I believe that you were going to change and it will take time and no matter how long I would wait for you. As for the baby, I found out a few weeks after I left. I wanted to tell you but I needed you to change for you and not because of the baby or us. I started saying change to be a family man, but you never caught it."

She took a deep breath and continued, "I had been visiting Mudcat, and I could only cry for he is somewhat paying for our mistakes. He knew you would hurt him, and I told him that I would not tell you unless he kept up with his lying. He agreed but I never knew what he was telling you about a woman he met. I have never slept with Mudcat and when you accused me of having his baby I wanted to scream it's yours, but something would not let me. I love you but you loved the streets more. I could not compete with what you have been doing all your life."

"Solo I love you and I have changed. It's never too late for us to work past this. I am equally sorrowful for Mudcat. I wish I could undo what is done but I can't. I can only learn from it."

The dispatcher came and said to Solo, "You have five more minutes."

Solo looked back at the lady and said, "Ok."

I asked Solo, "How did we go from good to bad?"

She looked at me and said, "The streets. You stayed faithful to them then you were to me."

There was no denying it. Solo was right. Then she said, "You all think that dick runs the nation but news flash, pussy births it. I got tired of you playing me for such a fool, sleeping with this woman, supporting that one and playing games with others so I decided to play you both for a fool. You see Mudcat is inexperienced with women, and he lets pussy run him. Your boy the one you trust so much is like a fish out of water; put him on dry land and all he will do is flap around here and there. He doesn't know shit and won't ever be shit without someone guiding him. He has always prized everything in your possession, even me. You never noticed the way he smiles when I am around. He wants to be you so bad that it literally made him green with envy, not dollar sign green but jealous green. That is why I got out of your way and got in his, by saying all the shit you men tell us when we are hurt, lonely and confused. How does it feel now to be on the receiving end of bullshit?"

I said, "These streets just don't make you cry, that bitch will make you kill."

Solo placed the receiver down and walked away.

EPILOGUE

L. T. spent five years on probation for the assault on Mudcat. He got out and did community service and stayed faithful to his wife. Their daughter was born the day Mudcat died. They paid for all his funeral expenses. The court decided not to indict him because Mudcat was trying to break up their home.

Solo and L. T. stayed together and nothing else ever came between them. They went on and three more children and raised them all Godly.

www.ingramcontent.com/pod-product-compliance
Lightning Source LLC
Chambersburg PA
CBHW032029240626
47154CB00003B/845